A
TOXIC
CRAFT

Debra Purdy Kong

Happy reading!

Debra Purdy Kong

A TOXIC CRAFT
Evan Dunstan Mystery #2

www.debrapurdykong.com

FIRST EDITION Trade Paperback

December 6, 2017

Published by Imajin Qwickies®, an imprint of Imajin Books®

www.ImajinQwickies.com

ISBN: 978-1-77223-340-7

Cover designed by Ryan Doan: www.ryandoan.com

Chapter One

"Hurry up, Evvy," Gran said, nudging his arm. "We're late!"

Evan sighed. Normally, he welcomed speed in his new Dodge Charger, but not now.

"Gran, the road's slushy and the Christmas tree's sliding forward."

He wished he'd had time to secure the damn thing to the roof better, but Gran and her cronies had badgered him relentlessly to get moving.

"Look out!" Gran yelled. "That car's crossing the centre line!"

As Evan swerved onto the shoulder, the

oncoming white compact veered back into the correct lane. It was too dark to see the driver clearly, but Evan glimpsed a bald head fringed in white.

Gran shook her fist at the driver. "You stupid son-of-a-whore!"

"Whoa." Evan glanced at her. "That's harsh."

"I'm eighty-one, Evvy. I can say whatever I want. And I've heard worse out of your mouth, Mister Smarty Pants."

"I learned from the best," he mumbled.

"I hope you mean your mother, young man."

Granted, Mom could curse with the best of them when provoked, but Evan had a pretty good idea who'd exposed her to the hard-core vocabulary.

"You shouldn't give Evan a hard time," Agnes said from the back seat. "He's doing us a huge favour by driving us back and forth all weekend."

A favour Evan had come to regret. Agnes had already spilled coffee in his car. Almost as annoying were Flo's knitting needles clacking right behind his head. Had he made a big mistake by suggesting that they hold the Christmas craft fair at

Southwest Trades & Technology's gymnasium? Gran had been so upset after the water pipe ruptured at the seniors' centre that Evan felt compelled to help. As second-in-command of security, he knew the campus gym was available. Final exams were nearly over, so parking wouldn't be a problem.

"I bet those flashing red and green lights in your hat distracted the driver," Flo remarked.

"Nonsense," Gran shot back. "The idiot driver was probably half asleep."

Agnes had a point, Evan thought. Decked out in her traditional elf costume, Gran was a blinking red and green embarrassment.

"For heaven's sake, Flo," Agnes said. "What's with the furious knitting?"

"Remember how quickly my bibs and booties sold out last year? I'm gonna outsell that demon Cora if it kills me."

Frowning, Evan said, "Who's demon Cora?"

"Cora Riddell," Flo answered for her. "A lousy knitter who's jealous of my skill and how much I sell. The evil creature lashes out anyway she can."

"Come on, Flo," Agnes said. "You provoke her and you know it."

"I do not."

"You *do*," Gran insisted.

"Are you two ganging up on me?" Flo's voice rose. "I thought you were my friends."

"We are, honey." Agnes patted her arm. "That's why we're telling you like it is."

Holy hell. Three days of this would drive him nuts. Evan pulled into STT and cruised past buildings and parking lots. Thank god it was too dark and the campus too empty to be seen with three old ladies and a big-ass Christmas tree.

"Oh, no. I was afraid this would happen," Gran grumbled. "A few vendors are already here. No one was supposed to show up till seven, but half of them never listen."

"The building's larger than I thought," Agnes said.

"You're only using the gym," Evan replied. "The other half is the weight room, fitness centre, and racquet ball courts."

The bike patroller, Steve, rode up to the small group of vendors. Evan sighed. Flo wasn't the only one who had issues with rivals. For the past eight months, Steve had made it clear to anyone who'd listen that he didn't think Evan deserved his promotion to second-in-command. Everyone knew that Steve thought he should have gotten the job.

"Crap!" Flo exclaimed. "The demon's here."

"Which one is she?" Evan asked.

"Flaming red hair, green hat, and purple coat," Gran replied. "She looks like a giant eggplant."

When Steve opened the gym door, Evan's jaw clenched. He'd left explicit instructions with the graveyard shift not to unlock the gymnasium until Evan called.

"He shouldn't be letting them in," Gran said. "We need to set up first."

"Steve's never been great with instructions," Evan muttered.

"So," Agnes remarked, "let the games begin."

"You mean the battle, don't ya?" Flo remarked.

"Shush," Gran said. "You'll worry Evvy."

Too late. Trepidation squirmed through Evan. Gran had assured him that this would be a smooth event, but he was beginning to have doubts. Evan stepped out of the car.

Steve rode up to him, stopping only inches from his door.

"You're running a seniors' shuttle service now?" He smirked. "My granny could use a lift to the mall later."

"Why did you open the gym door when I instructed guards to wait for the call?"

The smirk faded. "The old folks were complaining about the cold. What's the big deal?"

"Ignoring my instructions for the third time this week is the *big deal*."

"Evvy, bring the lights and decorations in with the tree!" Gran yelled from the steps.

"Better get moving, *Evvy*." Steve grinned.

An old gal pulling a loaded wagon approached them. "You security?" She looked from one to the other.

"Yes, ma'am," Evan answered. Given the size of her enormous eyeglasses, how could she not see the big *Security* lettering on his and Steve's bright yellow jackets?

"You need to do something about the ice in the parking lot. If I hadn't been gripping my cart, I could have fallen and broken a bone. That's serious at my age, you know."

"Sorry about that," Evan replied. "We'll

deal with it right away." He turned to Steve. "Get some rock salt from the storage shed."

"No time." He smirked. "Shift ends in ten minutes."

Fury scuttled through Evan. "Twelve by my watch. You can ride there and back in five, take a couple more minutes to sprinkle the salt, then make it back to HQ in time."

"Seriously? I don't remember you working that fast when you were a bike patroller."

Evan glared at him. "If you ignore instructions again, I'll write you up."

As expected, the smug condescension vanished. Guards loathed written warnings for various infractions. It wasn't just the humiliation, but the potential impact on performance reviews and pay raises.

Steve pedaled away, muttering, "Douche bag."

Evan fantasized about running him over with the Charger, then backing up and doing it again. He hauled the tree up the steps and into the lobby. Gran was placing her inflatable Santa at one end of the table and her homemade elf—dressed exactly like her—at the other end. Several feet behind her, two women were draping white cloths over two long tables, where the food would be sold.

"Gran, could you ask the volunteers to move the tables away from the trophy cases? I don't want any glass broken."

"The tables need to be near the outlet for the portable stove, Evvy." She placed a cash box on the table. "The tree goes on the tarp we placed just inside the gym door. The stand's there too."

Angry shouts erupted from inside the gym, but Gran and the volunteers kept working.

"What's going on?" Evan asked.

"Flo and Cora are arguing, but don't worry. They do this every year," Gran answered, as she kept working. "They'll get it together once the customers arrive."

Evan sure hoped so. He hauled the tree into the gym and spotted Flo pointing a knitting needle at Cora. Evan laid the tree on the tarp.

"If you try to sabotage my sales this year, Cora, I swear to god I'll stab you with my needle!"

"Just try it, you pathetic old hag!"

Holy shit. Evan marched toward them. "Ladies! This campus has a zero tolerance policy for any type of threat or harassment." He zeroed in on Flo. "It means you can't threaten anyone, understand?"

"Yeah." Flo glowered at Cora. "Fine."

As Cora turned to Evan, he inhaled sharply. Oh, hell no. The red hair, big pink cheeks, and glassy blue eyes bore a disturbing resemblance to the hideous doll a crazy ex-girlfriend used to carry in her purse. After he dumped the girl, the damn doll occasionally appeared on his doorstep or on the hood of his car. Although it hadn't happened in months, the memory still creeped him out.

Evan cleared his throat. "I'm Evan Dunstan."

"I know who you are." She crossed her arms. "Are you going to screw me over, too?"

"Sorry?"

"For starters, Martha stuck me at the back of the room *again*! Anything you can do about that?"

"I don't think so."

"Then you're no bloody good, are ya?"

Walk away, he told himself. "Excuse me. I need to set up the tree."

"I'm sure your darling grandmother's

told you that I'm the villain, but let me tell *you* that she, Flo, and Agnes have plenty to answer for!"

Evan kept going, not daring to turn around. A tall, gray-haired man in a bow tie and tweed vest came up to Evan.

"Don't mind Cora," he said. "Her bark's worse than her bite." He extended his hand. "Name's Walter. Martha told us that you're in charge of security at our little fair."

"Yes. We'll make sure the gym's locked up after vendors leave."

"Good to know." Walter paused. "I sell wooden bowls. They'd make a great gift for Martha, seeing as how she's always admired them."

"Thanks. I'll keep that in mind."

"Here. Let me hold the stand while you maneuver the tree in."

"Thanks." As they worked, Evan spotted Cora waddling toward the end of the room. "I heard that Flo and Cora have a tumultuous history."

"True. Those two get a little crazier every year. I used to think it was menopause, but they're way past that. It's just plain meanness now. You're in for a hell of a weekend, son."

Evan was afraid of that.

Chapter Two

New guard Felix Pennington's anxious voice blasted over the two-way radio, "Alpha Three to Alpha One?"

How many times had Evan told Felix not to hold the radio so close to his mouth that he was practically kissing the damn thing? Turning from his computer screen, he pressed the mic button. "Go ahead."

"There's a problem with the floor mats in the gym. Some of them aren't taped down properly and they're wrinkling," Felix said. "And there's a fender bender in the parking lot. Two old farts look like they're about to punch each other out."

Evan winced. Dispatchers, guards, the first-aid attendant, and security director, Okeyo Abasi, had all just heard Felix's less than professional reference to visitors. Okeyo would soon be telling Evan to review radio protocol with employees.

"Ten-four. En route."

Evan suddenly smiled. Thanks to a last-minute sick call, Steve was still on duty until a replacement could be found.

Evan pressed the mic button. "Alpha One to Alpha Two?"

As usual, Steve took his time responding. "Go ahead."

"Meet me in the gym ASAP, and bring duct tape."

"Shouldn't we call facilities about the mats?"

Evan rolled his eyes. "I spoke with them an hour ago. There's only one man on duty today, and he's busy dealing with a leak in the dorm. We'll have to handle things ourselves."

"Ten-four," Steve grumbled.

Evan headed toward the front of the security building, where the dispatch centre was located. One of the communications officers was on the phone. The second guy monitored four large, wall-mounted screens that were large enough to display thirty-two CCTV images at once.

"Hey," he said to the second officer. "Did you catch the fender bender on camera?"

"Yep. The SUV was backing up, but the driver in the sedan either didn't see him or didn't want to wait. I bookmarked the footage."

"Thanks. Keep camera six on the parking lot and seven on the gym's front entrance."

Too bad only two cameras monitored three sides of the building's exterior and adjoining parking lot. The far side had no coverage, which normally wasn't an issue since the back exit was rarely used. This weekend would be different. With a hundred vendors unloading supplies, both entrances would be needed.

Evan started out the door and nearly bumped into Cecelia. "Hi, beautiful." In the few months they'd been together, his girlfriend's gorgeous green eyes still took his breath away. "How's the studying going?"

"Terrible. This last final on Monday will

be the worst, and I haven't even thought about what to pack for the flight home."

Evan didn't want to hear about packing. He'd asked Cecelia to spend Christmas with him and his family, but her parents insisted that she return to Calgary and stay until the second of January. It killed him that she wouldn't be around for New Year's Eve.

"Are you free for coffee?" Cecelia asked.

"I wish, but there's a problem at the craft fair."

"Can I tag along? I planned to go anyway and say hi to Martha."

"Sure." Evan didn't quite understand why Gran and Cecelia had hit it off from the get-go, but he was grateful. Gran had helped his mom see what a wonderful woman Cecelia was.

One of the perks of his job was access to the security vehicle and the ability to park anywhere he wanted. The drive to the gym took all of sixty seconds. Evan stopped near the stairs and put on the flashers.

"Martha needn't have worried about customers not finding the new location," Cecelia said, scanning the vehicles. "The lot's packed."

At the top of the steps, Evan spotted a bag of rock salt and a hatchet propped against the wall near the door. Why the hell was a hatchet there? He tucked the tool behind the waste bin further down the wall. He'd take it to the vehicle on his way out.

Inside, Gran and Agnes were busy tending to customers.

Next to Gran, a plump woman in a red and black plaid top was saying, "Martha, she's really unhappy with me. I think it's best if I traded tables with someone."

"I can't deal with this right now, Marinde." Gran waved her hand dismissively. "I'll come see you later."

The woman's puffy cheeks reddened. She turned and headed inside the gym.

"You should give her a break, Martha," Agnes said. "That poor woman's always stuck next to—"

"Cecelia!" Gran exclaimed. "How are you, sweetheart?"

"Good, thanks. How much does it cost to get in?"

"Two dollars."

"A bargain." Cecelia handed over a toonie.

"No fair," a customer grumbled. "She

butted in."

"Why are you surprised?" her companion answered. "Martha has her favourites."

Gran appeared not to have heard them as she turned to Evan. "Are you here about the mat problem? We've got a room full of people with canes and walkers, Evvy. It needs to be dealt with."

"On it." He glanced at the door. "Has the other guard shown up?"

"You mean that little effeminate boy with the blue bangs?"

"No, that's Felix. I meant the guy on the bike who was here this morning."

"Oh. The snotty one." Gran's nose crinkled like she'd just smelled something bad. "Haven't seen him." She turned to Cecelia. "Take a look at our Christmas tree when you go inside. I persuaded the committee to use a real tree this year instead of that dusty old artificial thing. Our art class made gorgeous origami decorations."

"Can't wait to see it," Cecelia said.

In the gym, Evan gaped at hordes of shoppers at nearly every table. A few forlorn looking husbands dangled purses and bags over their arms. Flattening the floor mats would be a challenge, but not impossible. Each mat was only four by six feet, and clearly the duct tape was missing in places.

"Wow." Cecelia's fingertips grazed the tree's colourful ornaments. "They made the cutest reindeer and snowmen, and look at the tiny wreaths!"

A senior struggled to lift her walker over a rippled mat.

Evan hurried up to her and assisted in maneuvering past it. He tried stomping the ripple, but it wasn't working. Where in bloody hell was Steve?

"Need some help?" a familiar voice asked.

Evan looked up and smiled at his friend, Sully. "What brings you here?"

"Just finished an exam and didn't want to go home. Thought I'd check out the fair."

"Could you grab one end? We have to flatten this thing out."

"Sure." As Sully bent down, he grinned. "Who knew that this would be the best day of my life?"

"Why's that?" Evan took the other corner, grateful that shoppers were patient enough to stay back while they fixed the mat.

"I met a girl named Sydney. She helps her mom sell soaps and stuff."

"Cool." The short and chubby Sully rarely dated. As a plumbing student, he didn't meet that many girls either. Boosting his friend's confidence had become a challenging work in progress, but Evan hadn't given up on him. "You gonna ask her out?"

"Thought I'd start with coffee first. What do ya think?"

"Smart. If it goes well, ask her to lunch in the cafeteria."

Sully's head bobbed up and down. "Bold move. You should meet her."

"I will as soon as I finish checking the mats. Steve should be here any minute, so thanks for your help."

"No problem." As Sully left, Evan approached Cecelia who was admiring an amethyst necklace.

"This is stunning," she murmured.

Perfect. Evan had been wondering what to buy her for Christmas.

"Are you shopping or working?" Steve asked, tossing a roll of duct tape at him.

Cecelia stared at Steve, then, giving Evan a quick smile, wandered away. She didn't like the guy any better than he did.

"I've been waiting for you." *Asshole.* "Did you, by any chance, leave a hatchet next to salt bag ?"

"Yeah. Thought it might come in handy to bust icy potholes. Salt would take too long."

"Okay, but leaving it out in the open is dangerous with so many people around. I put it behind the waste bin."

"Good for you," Steve shot back.

Since the guy looked exhausted and was doing the team a favour by agreeing to the overtime, Evan kept his mouth shut. Making their way toward the back of the room, he spotted customers talking with Walter. No one was at Cora Riddell's table. Gaping at customers, she sipped from a blue water bottle.

"Hey, Five-O!" Sully called out. "Come meet Sydney!"

Sully beckoned Evan to the *Natural Scents* table that was perpendicular to Cora's. Ample space between the two tables allowed vendors access to the hallway that led to the washrooms and the back entrance.

"Gotta use the bathroom," Steve said, and hurried off.

Evan studied the short, plump girl wrapping colourful soaps in tissue paper. Next to her, was the woman in red and black whom Gran had brushed off earlier. Sydney's eyes bulged a little too much in her round face, and the Christmas sweater with the reindeer antlers hanging off her chest was just weird.

After Sully introduced them, Sydney said, "How come Sully calls you Five-O?"

Evan and Sully exchanged grins. He figured that Sully was hoping she'd ask. "After Sully's family arrived from Vietnam, he taught himself English by watching TV crime shows," Evan answered. "As it turned out, he and I solved a real-life murder on campus a few months back. Sully's a smart guy."

While her face filled with admiration, her mother's darkened with disapproval. Evan had no way of telling if it was because he'd mentioned a murder or that the lady didn't like Sully.

"You'll have to tell me about it," Sydney said to Sully.

Sully beamed. "I could do that, if you're free for coffee. I mean, I know you're busy right now. But maybe later?"

"Awesome! Could you show me around the campus? I need to take some science courses if I want to become a veterinarian's assistant."

"I love animals!" Sully said.

Sydney's big eyes lit up. "Do you have any pets?"

"No. My father doesn't like animals or people that much."

Sydney sighed. "I know the feeling."

Sully turned to Evan. "You should buy some soaps for Cecelia and your mom. And your grandma probably deserves something nice."

"You sure about that?" Cora said right behind Evan. "'Cause she's doing an even shittier job than usual."

Evan flinched. Man, just like that damn doll, the woman popped up where she wasn't wanted. Her glassy eyes blinked at him exactly the same way.

"Those tree decorations look stupid, and how hard would it have been to switch tables with me and that sleaze-bag, Flo?" Cora took a gulp from her water bottle . "I told Martha that I'm becoming allergic to Marinde's soaps. Some people have sensitivities, you know."

Cora glared at Marinde, who smiled at an approaching customer. Sydney, on the other hand, scowled at Cora until Sully took her hand and asked when she'd be free for coffee.

"Mrs. Riddell, you have a customer," Evan said.

The old bat turned and scurried back to her table just as Steve returned.

"Are you gonna yak all day or are you going to help fix these mats?" Steve frowned. "Are you sure you can handle being in charge of this thing?"

Evan was about to fire back a response when a woman further down the aisle shouted, "Help!"

A cluster of people bent down. Shit. Someone had fallen. Evan edged his way through the gawkers to find a woman about his mom's age sitting on the floor. One of her slip-on shoes had come off.

Evan bent down. "Ma'am, are you hurt?"

"No. I'm fine." Peering up at him, she grinned. "Martha was right. You are a cutie, and tall too."

Terrific. Did every damn person here know that he was related to Gran? "Let me help you up."

"It's that mat," the woman said, taking his hand. "It's all bunched up."

"We've been working on flattening them out," Evan said. "Sorry that we didn't get to this one in time."

"No worries, son. You're doing your best under what must be challenging circumstances."

Evan helped the woman to her feet. "Are you sure you're okay? We have a first-aid attendant on duty."

"Oh my, that's not necessary. It's just a little stumble." Keeping a grip on Evan's arm, the lady slid her foot into her shoe. "You know, your thick, dirty-blond hair reminds me of my husband in his glory days. And the baby face is most becoming."

"Yeah." Steve smirked. "That's what we all say."

Asshole. "Let's flatten this mat properly," Evan said.

Disdain flashed across Steve's face until he noticed that several customers were watching him. Evan asked them to stand back, then bent down and got to work. They were nearly done when Cecelia reappeared.

"Sully just introduced me to Sydney,"

she murmured to Evan. "He seems truly smitten."

"Yeah, that was my impression. What do you think of her?"

Cecelia's perfect brows puckered. "A tiny bit odd which makes her perfect for Sully. Think we should double-date sometime?"

"Not ever."

Cecelia chuckled. "I should get back to studying."

"Call you later."

After they'd fixed all of the mats, a bleary-eyed Steve said, "I'm gonna see if dispatch has found a replacement for me yet."

He didn't wait for Evan's response, not that Evan expected him to. Now that he was alone, he ventured toward the table selling the amethyst necklace and earring set. It was still there and about fifty bucks more than he'd planned to spend, but Cecelia was worth it. He paid with a credit card and asked the vendor to hold it for him.

On his way out of the gym, Evan glanced at Flo who was talking with a happy, animated expression and holding up her products for a customer. At least she was having a good time.

In the lobby, Agnes chatted with volunteers while Gran tidied the table and adjusted her elf.

"Just out of curiosity," he whispered to her, "you've got proper insurance coverage, right?"

Gran peered up at him, her face suspicious. "What happened?"

"A customer tripped and fell over one of the rippled mats, but she's okay. They're all fixed now."

"Good. All the paper work's been done on the insurance, so relax, Evvy. You look stressed."

Evan was tempted to say, why wouldn't he be? When it came to paperwork, Gran had a talent for skipping important details. His parents had learned this the hard way after she sideswiped Dad's car—which had been parked on the street—and didn't bother to tell him. They learned the truth when the insurance company called to ask why Gran missed her appointment with the adjustor. That's when Mom decided that Gran would no longer drive, and how he found himself playing chauffeur this weekend.

"Hi, Evan." Felix joined them.

"I don't believe we've officially met," Gran said. "I'm Martha Dunstan, the craft fair's organizer."

"Felix Pennington, new patrol officer." He looked at her outfit, then glanced at the elf. "Love the matching outfits. Did you make them?"

"I did, and I love your blue bangs. Are you in a band?"

"No. I do makeup for theatre groups. Planning to work in TV and movies."

Gran smiled. "Maybe I should add some colour to my hair. How about hot pink?"

"You'd look fabulous," Felix said.

Evan frowned. This conversation was going way off track.

"Felix, patrol the gym once an hour, and be sure to watch for any other issues with the mats."

"No problem."

Right. Straight from the newbie who'd been at this job a whole four weeks. If something went wrong, vendors like Cora Riddell would eat Felix alive.

Chapter Three

As Evan finished the last of his paperwork for the day, Felix's anxious voice once again blasted over the radio.

"Alpha Three to Romeo One," he yelled. "Code White in the women's washroom, back hallway!"

"Romeo One copies," the first-aid attendant, Gus, replied. "What's the situation?"

"A woman fell in the bathroom. She's breathing, but unconscious. I think we'll need an ambulance, but I'm not sure."

"Dispatch, I'll let you know about the ambulance as soon as I get there," Gus said.

"No point in calling until I can brief them on her condition."

"Ten-four."

Evan swore under his breath. His shift was due to end soon, but he couldn't leave during a medical emergency. He pressed the mic button. "Alpha One to Romeo One, I'll pick you up shortly."

"I'll be ready."

Since timing was crucial in emergencies, supervisors always drove first-aid attendants to the patient. Evan was just glad that STT's most experienced attendant was on duty. Medical personnel weren't usually around during final exam time, but considering the number of seniors estimated to attend the 3-day event, Evan had persuaded Okeyo to keep someone around.

Evan hurried outside. Less than a minute later, he pulled up to the first-aid building. As Gus hopped in the vehicle, Felix was on the radio again, telling them that the patient's pulse was slow.

"How slow?" Gus asked.

"Real slow."

Gus turned to Evan. "Did the new guy take the Occupational First Aid course?"

"Yeah, it's still mandatory," Evan

replied. "But Felix panics easily."

"No shit."

Since it was twenty minutes past four and the fair closed at four p.m., the parking lot was nearly empty. Evan pulled up to the gym's back entrance.

Inside, a handful of vendors stood at the end of the hallway. A tall, white-haired woman stepped away from the group, and with the aid of a cane, moved toward Evan.

"Cora's in there," she said, pointing to the women's room.

Evan's stomach clenched. "Cora Riddell?"

"The one and only."

Freaking wonderful. Evan followed Gus into the women's room and found Cora flat on her back, eyes closed. Felix was kneeling next to her, his expression fearful. When he saw Evan, relief swept over him.

"Did she come to at all?" Gus asked Felix.

"Sort of." Felix got to his feet. "She moaned a bit and those gaudy blue eyelids flickered."

"Sshh," Evan said. "She might hear you."

"Sorry, but that shade of blue only

belongs in porn flicks." Felix edged closer to Evan. "The woman nearly threw her water bottle at me for touching her merchandise earlier." He shook his head. "I never knew my grandparents, but aren't old people supposed to be nice? She's horrible!"

"Tell me about it," Evan mumbled. "Do you know if anyone saw what happened?"

"Not sure. But a lady with white hair and nice makeup found her."

"Does she use a cane?"

"Yeah."

Evan noticed a puddle of water around Cora's head. "Felix, was water on the floor when you came in?"

"Yeah. She must have slipped on it."

Cora opened her glassy doll-like eyes. Evan flinched.

"Didn't realize you were skittish," Gus said, and smiled.

"I'm not. It's just that she and I had words this morning," he mumbled.

Cora tried to sit up, then groaned.

"Lie still, ma'am," Gus said, easing her back down. "Are you feeling any pain?"

"My head hurts."

Gus looked at Evan. "Get an ambulance."

As Evan radioed dispatch, he caught sight of blinking red and green lights. Gran stepped inside, carrying a megaphone, of all things.

When he was done, he said, "What's with the megaphone?"

"To get peoples' attention in emergencies." She studied the still blinking Cora. "Any idea how she fell, Evvy?"

Gus smirked. "*Evvy?*"

"This is my grandmother. She's also the fair's organizer."

"Nice to meet you," Gus said to her.

"Likewise. Good to know that medical help's nearby."

Evan turned to Felix. "Head outside and watch for the ambulance."

"But my shift's over."

"Guards don't walk away during code calls, Felix—*ever.* You'll be paid overtime."

"Okay." Felix scurried out of the room, as if he couldn't get out of there fast enough.

Evan ushered Gran out the door as well. "Where were Flo and Agnes when Cora fell?" he asked.

"Agnes was helping Flo cover her table for the night." Gran peered at him. "You don't think they had anything to do with

Cora's fall, do you? It was just an accident."

"Yeah. Probably." Flo's angry threat this morning meant he had to consider all possibilities, though. Maybe others had issues with demon Cora. "I'm just trying to find out if anyone witnessed the fall." He spotted the tall, white-haired woman chatting with Walter. "Who's the woman with the cane?"

"Janelle. She was the fair's organizer before me."

"She's the one who found Cora. I need to talk to her."

"Figures she'd be in the thick of it."

"Why's that?"

"Because she enjoys being the centre of attention," Gran muttered. "Likes to stir things up."

"Does she get along with Cora?"

"Better than most." Gran stared at the woman. "Hmm. Janelle's face is splotchy, which is odd since she usually has beautiful skin, thanks to Marinde's soaps. We all swear by them, you know. I should pick up some tomorrow."

Evan rolled his eyes. "Can we focus, please? I need to talk to potential witnesses before everyone leaves."

"On it." Gran stepped into the gym and raised the megaphone. "Attention, vendors! As you know, my grandson's in charge of security and he needs to talk to anyone who might have seen Cora fall in the can."

Evan cringed. He would have preferred more discretion. A few vendors gawked at Gran like she'd sprouted a second nose. Others ignored her as they continued tidying their tables. Sydney and Marinde gave him sympathetic glances.

"Can you hear me?" Gran's voice rose. "Is this thing on?"

"Gran, the whole campus can hear you."

As Gran approached Janelle, Walter headed back to his table.

"My grandson needs to ask you some questions."

"I'm sure he does," Janelle answered. "Thank you, Martha."

Judging from Gran's fierce expression, Janelle's patronizing smile pissed her off. Evan stepped in front of Gran. "Can you make sure the hallway stays clear of people? The paramedics'll need to get the gurney inside."

"Sure thing, Evvy."

Marinde walked up to Evan, her arms

loaded with empty boxes. He noticed that Sydney was busy straightening their products.

"I don't mean to trouble you," Marinde said, "but would it be okay if I left through the back entrance? It's much closer to my van."

"Of course." Evan turned to Gran. "Let the vendors who are ready to leave use the back door."

"Gotcha." She raised the damn megaphone. "Those who want to leave through the back should do so now, and watch your step, folks. We don't need another accident."

Evan shrugged at Janelle. "Sorry about that."

"No worries. I've worked with Martha a long time, and know how attached she is to the megaphone."

Evan smiled as he retrieved his notebook. "Do you know what time you found Mrs. Riddell?"

"Let's see. I was helping Walter with last minute customers, then went to use washroom at about ten past four. I found Cora unconscious on the floor."

"Was anyone else in the bathroom?"

"Not that I saw, though I suppose someone could have been in one of the stalls. I left to get help right away."

As Evan jotted her answer down, Walter rejoined them.

"Terrible thing," he said. "Poor Cora doesn't have much luck."

"Do you mean that she's fallen before?" Evan asked.

"Yes," he answered, "but that's not unusual. Balance diminishes with age, and I heard that she had some vertigo issues a while back."

Then it probably was an accident. Still…"Did you happen to see Mrs. Riddell leave her table?" Evan asked. "Or notice who else might have gone down the hall around closing time?"

"Sorry, son. Janelle and I were wrapping bowls for customers."

"Maybe one of the other vendors saw something." Janelle glanced at the empty tables next to Walter. "Looks like some have already left for the day."

That's what worried Evan. At that time, no one would have paid much attention to Cora's whereabouts. By tomorrow, memories would have faded.

"Wait," Janelle said. "Now that I think about it, I do remember seeing a woman head out the exit just as I entered the hallway."

"Who?" Evan asked.

Janelle's gaze darted from one side of the room to the other, as if worried about being overheard. "Agnes."

"Oh." Why would she have been at this end of the gym when she was supposed to be helping Flo? Evan looked toward the other end of the room. Flo and Agnes were fiddling with a sheet draped over Flo's knitted goods. "Who was nearby when you called for help?"

"Not many. Marinde Marchant was the only one who bothered to ask what was wrong."

Evan glanced at the *Natural Scents* table, surprised to see that Sully had shown up.

"I'm afraid that's all I know," Janelle said.

"Thanks for your time."

Evan approached Sully and told him about Cora's accident.

"Is she all right?" Sydney asked, her expression pensive.

"She's semi-conscious, but if she hit her head, there could be a concussion," Evan answered. "Did you see Cora head down the hallway around closing time?"

Sydney hesitated. "I caught a glimpse of someone going down the hall. She kind of looked like that lady down there." She pointed to Flo's table.

"Do you mean the taller or shorter one?"

"The shorter one, "Sydney answered.

Agnes. Evan sighed.

Marinde returned and picked up more empty boxes. Evan asked if she'd seen Agnes in the hall.

"Sorry, but I didn't see anything." Marinde paused. "Cora was complaining about feeling lightheaded an hour ago. She said it gets worse in warm, crowded rooms like this one. It's partly why she's always assigned a spot by a door. A little fresh air wafting in is better than nothing."

Janelle was right. All those customers had made it overly warm in here. Evan jotted down more notes when Gran announced that the ambulance was here. Evan greeted the paramedics and ushered them into the washroom. Gran started to follow him inside, but he didn't want her hanging about.

"Gran, can you make sure the hallway stays clear and no one comes in?"

"No problem, Evvy."

As she left, Evan whispered to Gus, "I just heard that Cora was feeling lightheaded and that she's had a vertigo problem."

"It could explain the fall." Gus gave him a strange look. "Thing is, the lady insists that someone pushed her."

Chapter Four

The fifteen minute drive to STT was
unusually quiet this morning. Although
Evan still heard the irritating clack of Flo's
knitting needles and the unappealing slurp of
Agnes's coffee, chatter was nonexistent. No
surprise, he supposed.

Although Evan lived in the converted,
detached garage at the back of his parents'
property, he often shared meals with them.
Popping in for breakfast this morning, he
caught the end of a conversation between
Mom and Gran. It seemed the cops had
spoken with Gran last night about Cora
Riddell, however Gran was less than

forthcoming about the details. All she would tell him was that they asked if she'd seen what happened and if anyone might want to hurt Cora.

"What did you tell them?" Evan had asked.

"What was I supposed to say, Evvy?" Gran replied with a huff. "Half of the vendors want to kill her, but I'm not about to tell the cops that."

Although Evan hadn't told Gran that Cora claimed she'd been pushed, he did so at that time. It hadn't helped. In fact, Gran became less forthcoming. When he told her that two witnesses saw Agnes heading down the back hallway after Cora, Gran got all pissed and told him he was flat out wrong. Insisted that Agnes had been helping Flo the whole time.

"How can you be sure?" he'd asked. "You weren't with them constantly."

"Agnes always helps Flo," she argued. "It's their routine, and one doesn't mess with Flo's routine if they know what's good for them."

Once her cronies arrived, Gran refused to discuss the issue any further on the drive to STT. Too bad for her, because Evan still needed answers, and since he had a captive audience…

"Ladies, did Gran tell you that the cops called her about Cora last night?"

The clacking knitting needles stopped. "What?" Flo leaned forward until she was breathing down Evan's neck. "What did they want?"

"To find out what happened to Cora," he added, noticing that Gran was looking out the side window. "They asked if Gran knew anyone who would want to hurt her."

"Martha! Why didn't you phone us?" Agnes asked.

"'Cause it was nothing," she grumbled, then glared at Evan. "Still is."

"Martha," Flo said, her tone wary, "what did you tell them?"

"That everyone got along and things are fine."

Agnes laughed. "In other words, you lied your ass off. Good girl."

"What if she's caught in that lie?" Evan said. "I wasn't the only one who heard you threaten Cora yesterday, Flo. It seems the animosity between you is well known."

"So what?" Gran shot back. "No one could have seen Flo at that end of the room 'cause she was busy with customers, then tidying her display. And the cops didn't say anything about Cora claiming that she was pushed, so don't go pointing fingers, mister."

"She said that?" Agnes said. "What a bitch!"

"Oh, dear," Flo said. "The cops will want to talk to me, won't they?"

"Possibly."

"It doesn't matter," Agnes replied. "Neither of us were anywhere near that bathroom when Cora fell. Hell, I didn't even know there were bathrooms down there, so we're in the clear."

Evan saw the warning in Gran's eyes, the one that said *don't you dare mention the witnesses who'd claimed to see Agnes follow Cora down the hall.*

"Cora will find a way to blame me," Flo mumbled.

"Don't worry," Gran said. "You know she likes to make up stories to cause trouble. Anyone the cops interview will tell them that."

"I take it the police didn't contact other vendors?" Agnes asked.

Gran adjusted her blinking red and green

hat. "They wanted a list, so I emailed mine."

"I hope the cops don't show up at the fair," Flo remarked. "That could be bad for business."

"Don't worry about it," Agnes replied. "It shouldn't take them long to figure out that Cora Riddell is a hostile, paranoid nut case with big grudges and health issues. That's exactly what I'll tell them if they approach me. I know a dozen other vendors who'll vouch for every word I say."

Evan sighed. Would the police see it that way, though?

"With Cora in the hospital, at least we'll have a peaceful day," Flo said.

"I sure as hell hope so," Gran replied.

Ditto, Evan thought.

He pulled up to the building's entrance, where Steve stood there, apparently waiting for them. Evan hoped he was only there to unlock the entrance and not report any trouble.

Evan followed Gran and her posse up the steps.

"Everything go okay last night?" he asked Steve.

Steve flashed a smile. "About how you'd expect." He unlocked the door, then took off.

Evan stepped over the threshold as Gran shouted, "What in holy hell?"

"Holiness has nothing to do with that," Flo shot back.

Agnes burst into a loud cackle at the sight of Santa lying on the table with the elf on top of him, its hands duct taped around Santa's neck.

"Sacrilege!" Gran shouted.

"Relax," Agnes replied as she and Flo headed for the gym. "It was probably just some students having a bit of fun." She turned to Evan. "Or that guard of yours. He looked a bit dodgy, the way he tore out of here."

True. Steve had better bloody not have been behind this. Evan had specifically requested that the door between the fitness centre and gym be secured at five p.m. The guard who'd been working last evening—an easygoing, older guy named Dave—never forgot to do the lockups.

Evan had just finished untaping the elf when Agnes came running into the lobby.

"Flo's table's been vandalized! Someone squirted mustard all over her products!"

Gran's mouth fell open as she gaped at

her friend, then started for the gym. Evan hurried after them and soon found himself staring at the slightly smudged yellow loops stretched along the table on top of several knitted items.

"Can you believe this?" Flo's face was scrunched with fury. "Thank god the stock under the table wasn't damaged."

"Evvy, you need to find out who did this," Gran said.

"It won't be easy. There's no cameras inside the building."

Of the eighty cameras on campus, only ten of them monitored indoor rooms, all of which were high security areas, not the gymnasium or its lobby. If the dispatchers had left the camera on the front entrance, Evan could view comings and goings. The back entrance was another matter, seeing as how the second camera was supposed to have been pointed at the parking lot.

"I hate to say it, Evvy, but what if one of the guards did this?" Gran asked. "You need to question them."

"I will." While Evan took photos of the damage, a horrible thought occurred to him. "Gran, maybe you should check the other tables."

"Oh, crap." Gran rushed to the nearest table. "Agnes, check the tables in the next aisle."

"This has to be Cora's doing," Flo muttered. "She must have gotten out of the hospital. Even if she didn't, she could have coerced or blackmailed someone into doing her dirty work."

Evan's eyebrows rose. "Blackmailed? Would she stoop that low?"

Flo's expression darkened. "You don't know Cora. When she wants something, she'll stop at nothing to get it. And she wants me out of these craft fairs permanently!"

If Cora had been here, it's possible that her image would appear on CCTV cameras.

Evan approached Gran. "Aside from Cora, does Flo have other enemies?"

"Not really." Gran lifted a sheet draped over jars of jams and jellies. "The other three knitters are jealous of her skill, but I can't believe they'd resort to this. One's obese and can barely walk, the second's in a wheelchair, and the third woman's so frail that I doubt that she has the strength to squirt mustard on a hot dog, let alone an entire table."

"You'll be blamed for this," Agnes said from across the aisle. "Your ability to run the fair will be called into question again."

Evan frowned at Gran. "What does she mean by *again*?"

"It's not important." Gran waved her hand dismissively. "We've got more immediate worries, like fixing everything before the customers show up."

"Hey, Evan?" Felix poked his head in the gym. "The supervisor sent me over to hurry you up for shift change. He wants to go home."

"Be there shortly. Do you know if Steve's still around?"

"No, he took off in a hurry," Felix replied. "Is this about the angry elf?"

"Yeah. I take it the topic came up during shift change?"

Felix chuckled. "Oh, yeah. Info was passed from Dave to Steve to me. No one knows who did it."

At least the guards followed protocol. Anything unusual was verbally communicated from one shift to the next and recorded in notebooks.

"Did either of those guys bother to take a photo, write an incident report, or even think to dismantle the display?" Evan asked.

"Well, they all took photos. I got a copy, which I'm turning into this year's Christmas card." Felix smirked. "And I think a report was written, but no one wanted to touch the display."

"Did anyone mention mustard smears?"

Felix frowned. "What?"

Evan beckoned him to Flo's table.

"Oh, my god! Who would do that? I was going to buy a bib and bootie set for my twin nieces."

"You still can," Flo said. "I have more stuff in bins under the table, and they've not been touched."

"Evvy, I've got to get things ready out front," Gran said, glancing at her watch. "Agnes will check the rest of the tables."

"Felix, give Agnes a hand, okay? We need to make sure that none of the other vendors were vandalized," Evan said. "I've got to get going."

"No problem."

As Evan and Gran entered the lobby, they saw Janelle and Walter chuckling at the elf and Santa.

"Love what you've done with the décor, Martha," Janelle said.

"What are you two doing here so early?" Gran retorted. "Unless you knew there'd be something to gawk at?"

Their amusement faded. Walter fidgeted and looked embarrassed. Janelle's face turned to stone.

"Just what are you implying, Martha?" Janelle asked.

"Everyone knows that you didn't want me taking over this fair. I can't help wondering if you want to make me look bad by pulling that juvenile stunt."

Janelle glared at her. "You actually believe I would do such a thing?"

"I'm sure you had your lover's help." Gran threw a meaningful look at Walter. "Seeing as how you never showed much initiative when you were the organizer."

Evan shook his head. Why was Gran provoking her? "Gran, the food volunteers look like they need help. How about you pitch in."

"Fine. Whatever, Evvy." Gran turned and stomped across the lobby.

"Come help me set up the new stock." Walter placed his hand on the small of Janelle's back.

"In a minute," she answered quietly, her

expression still rigid. "You go ahead."

Janelle turned to Evan. "Do you really think we'd pull a stupid prank on Martha?"

"Actually, this is more than a silly prank." Seeing as how Janelle and other vendors would soon find out anyway, he told her about the mustard.

"Oh, my." Janelle's hand covered her mouth. "Things are getting out of hand."

"Any idea who would want to do that?"

"No, and I hate to say it, but Flo may have created her own trouble." Janelle leaned heavily on her cane, her expression sombre. "You should know that she hasn't treated the other knitters very well."

Interesting. "What's she done?"

Janelle again looked at Gran, who was busy with the food vendors. Leaning closer to Evan, she whispered, "Flo stole another knitter's pattern idea, and last year she spilled water over a vendor's beautiful scarves. She claimed it was an accident, but everyone wondered."

Clearly, Janelle did.

"There were repercussions too," Janelle added. "On the final day of last year's fair, Flo found a sticky candy cane on one of her nicest baby blankets."

"Aside from the knitters, do you know if Flo has clashed with other vendors?"

Janelle looked at the gym's entrance. Evan could almost see her thoughts reeling. "Well, she is competitive and likes to boast about her sales. And yes, that offends some vendors, but I can't picture any of them resorting to that kind of damage."

Still, it would be interesting to know which vendors had been most offended by Flo's boasting.

"I have to say," Janelle went on, "that, despite what your grandmother thinks or says, I'm quite relieved not to be running this fair anymore. The vendors are a demanding bunch. But this year, the hostility has certainly reached a new destructive level."

Was Gran in over her head? Evan knew she was stressed, and now he'd have to confront her with awkward questions about Cora blackmailing folks and Flo offending far too many people.

Felix rushed into the lobby, out of breath. "Cora's table has been hit too!"

Evan looked at Janelle who looked as shocked as he felt.

"Damn it!" Gran scurried into the gym.

As Evan, Felix, and Janelle followed, he said, "Cora seems like the type who'd sue."

"Yes, but she wouldn't succeed," Janelle replied. "Before they're given a table, every vendor must sign a waiver agreeing not to take legal action in the event of lost, stolen, or damaged property. I assume STT has a similar policy?"

"Yes." Still, Okeyo wouldn't be happy. He'd expect Evan to identify the culprit.

Walter stood next to Cora's table, staring at the same type of mustard loops that had messed up Flo's display. Evan pulled out his phone and began snapping photos.

"I covered her table before I left last night," Walter said. "It was fine then."

"Guess that lets Mrs. Riddell off as a suspect," Felix murmured.

Good point. Evan turned to Gran. "This doesn't look like a guard or student prank. Any thoughts about vendors?"

Gran shrugged. "Cora's angered a lot of people."

"Can you narrow it down to vendors who've been pissed off with both of them?"

"Well, now. I'll have to think about that, Evvy."

"How would someone have pulled this off without being seen?" Felix said. "With all the commotion at closing time yesterday, it would have been hard for anyone to do that kind of damage unless they hid till everyone left."

"Where could they hide?" Gran asked.

"Maybe in the fitness centre, or in the washrooms just off the lobby," Evan replied. "The suspect could have grabbed one of the mustard bottles off the condiments table."

"You're right!" Felix replied. "And the volunteers might have been too busy cleaning up to notice."

Evan needed to find out when Dave had locked the door between the centre and the gym. He would have preferred that it stayed locked, but since the bathrooms were just inside the fitness centre, the door was propped open while the fair was open. He also wanted to talk to the food volunteers later. First, though, he needed to get to shift change.

"Evvy, please," Gran said. "You must find out who did this as soon as possible or the fair could be ruined!"

"I'll do my best." He had to.

An act of vandalism against the vendor

who'd already claimed that someone tried to harm her would definitely warrant police involvement. Given that Evan had applied to the RCMP and the first phase of the application process was underway, this was a chance to prove himself. Catching a killer eight months ago could be perceived as a fluke. Steve sure as hell thought so. Time to show everyone that it wasn't.

"Felix, I need you to stay here today and keep a close eye on things," Evan said. "I'll have the other guards patrol the rest of your zone."

Felix's eyes widened in horror. "You're going to leave me here with these old folks?"

"Yep. Don't worry, I'll be popping by a lot."

"This is a nightmare."

"Yeah," Evan mumbled. "Tell me about it."

Chapter Five

A large presence filled Evan's doorway. Without looking up, he knew who it was. No one filled a doorway like security director Okeyo Abasi. The boss rarely came in on a Saturday, but Evan wasn't surprised to see him. He'd emailed Okeyo incident reports about Cora's accident, the Santa prank, and the mustard vandalism.

Okeyo stepped inside and quietly closed the door. The orange plastic chair creaked as the big man sat down. Evan noted the sheets of paper in his hand.

"Are your grandmother's events always this problematic?"

Evan squirmed. "Not that I'd heard." He doubted that Gran had told him everything, though.

"The police haven't contacted me about the accident in the women's washroom. But that will likely change once the victim learns about the vandalism to her table."

"If we're lucky, she won't learn about it until the fair's over."

Okeyo's smile didn't meet his eyes. "Do you really think we'll have that kind of luck, Evan?"

He cringed. "Probably not."

Okeyo sighed. "If the police show up, let me know right away. Meanwhile, I want to discuss the timeline you mentioned in your report."

Evan figured he'd ask, which was why he'd gone over the guards' notebooks thoroughly and then called Steve and Dave.

"You've confirmed that Dave locked up the building and the door between the gym lobby and the fitness centre at 5:05 p.m.?"

"Yes. He was supposed to secure everything after the last person left, which would have been my grandmother and her friends."

"You stated that the paramedics left at

4:35." Okeyo turned a page of the sheets in his hand. "And that the last people left at 4:40 p.m."

"Yes."

"Then why didn't Dave lock up right after that?"

"He'd been called to open an office for a faculty member who couldn't find her office key." Evan cleared his throat. "Apparently, the woman wound up dumping the contents of her purse all over the floor. Dave helped her put everything back. Turned out she'd left the key in her office."

Okeyo shook his head. "From now on, there's to be no time lapse between the last person to leave the premises and securing the building. In fact, a guard should be present as the gym is clearing out."

Evan nodded. "Understood."

"I know the team doesn't normally patrol washrooms," Okeyo added. "But under the circumstances, I think they should."

"Okay." Evan cleared his throat. "I've just begun reviewing CCTV footage to see which vendors left through the front entrance."

"What about the back?"

"The camera was kept on the parking lot. All I can do is determine which vendors headed for their cars from that side of the building. I'm looking to see if any of them left between 4:40 and 5:05 p.m."

"Let me know if you find anything." Okeyo paused. "Do you think the same person pulled this morning's moronic stunt with Santa?"

Evan hesitated. "My gut tells me that it could be two different people. One act seems juvenile, while the other feels malicious and personal."

"If there are two, then are they working together?"

"I don't know." But it was an interesting idea.

"Then we'd better find out." Okeyo's deep baritone was ominously low. "Is it remotely possible that the Santa thing was a guard's doing?"

There was no dodging the question. The dark, penetrating eyes of Okeyo Abasi could decipher truth from lies in a heartbeat. "Maybe."

Okeyo clasped his hands together. "Which one would you put your money on?"

Man, he didn't want to be put in this position. "Well, I doubt it was Dave."

"What about Steve?"

Evan swallowed. He didn't like the guy, but finger-pointing was uncomfortable. "It's a possibility."

Okeyo didn't look surprised. "Review his notebook again carefully. See if there are passages of time where nothing's been written down. I want to know where he was every damn minute of his shift."

Okeyo was well aware that guards weren't required to record every minute of a building patrol, but they were required to call in once a minimum of three buildings had been patrolled. Some guards rushed through patrols so they could slack off or get up to mischief.

"Spend more time in the gym, Evan. The newbie can't handle everything on his own." Okeyo stood. "I'll be catching up on paperwork. Let's hope your seniors don't burn the place down before the damn fair's over."

"It won't happen. Don't worry."

The look Okeyo gave him suggested that worrying was inevitable. It also suggested that Evan had better not let him down.

Okeyo shut the door as Evan's cell phone rang.

"You won't believe this!" Gran sounded frantic. "Cora's back and she's heading for her table! I haven't had time to put her damaged stuff away."

"Oh, shit. Why would she even bother? It's two o'clock."

"When you need money as badly as she does, even one sale helps," Gran replied. "There'll be a shitstorm when she sees that mess, Evvy. Better come quick 'cause I don't think that little guard Felix can handle her."

"On my way."

Evan was tempted to warn Felix, but the thought of every guard and Okeyo—who always kept a radio on—hearing about more trouble was too embarrassing. Grabbing his jacket, Evan rushed out the door.

Two minutes later, he was forced to wait for a group of slow-moving seniors to enter the building. Sighing impatiently, he glanced at the waste bin, then did a double take. The bag of rock salt was still there, but the hatchet was gone. He'd forgotten to pick it up yesterday, so where the hell was it? Evan moved toward the bin and peered behind it. Nothing. He checked the adjoining recycling bins. Still nothing. Damn. Had Steve removed the hatchet, or had someone else?

Inside, Evan spotted Agnes at the registration table, urgently waving him over.

"Martha's in the gym, trying to calm Cora down," Agnes said. "You know your grandmother's terrible at that, right?"

"Hell yeah."

Evan charged ahead, entering a gymnasium that was noisier and more crowded than ever.

He maneuvered his way toward the back, where Cora was shrieking, "You and Flo will pay for this, Martha, I swear!"

Evan marched past Walter's table. Walter seemed to be trying hard to ignore them as he straightened his bowls. Janelle, on the other hand, appeared bemused by the spectacle. Some customers gawked at Cora and Gran. Others hurried away.

Felix rushed up, flicking blue bangs out of his eyes. "That crazy redhead told me to call cops. Do you think I should?"

"Not yet. Let me talk to her."

As Evan edged closer, he noted Cora's lopsided tuque and the unruly hair sticking out in all directions. Had she been released from the hospital or had she just left?

"Mrs. Riddell?" Evan moved closer to Gran. "I'm sorry to hear about your table. Can we help you remove the damaged items?"

"You can help me identify the piece of filth who did this to my beautiful knitting!"

"I intend to."

"Yeah. Right." She crossed her arms. "I bet you're conspiring with Martha against me."

"He is not," Gran shot back.

"I'm concerned about your well-being." Evan kept his voice calm. "After yesterday's fall, are you sure you're well enough to be here?"

"How *dare* you insult me!" She raised her hand.

Felix gasped.

"She's lost her friggin' mind," Gran muttered.

"I'm not trying to insult you, Mrs. Riddell. I'm just worried about your health. My understanding is that you sustained a concussion yesterday."

"I'm not discussing my medical condition with you." Cora kept her hand raised. "Mind your own business!"

"Mrs. Riddell," Evan warned, taking a step back. "Hitting anyone will result in an immediate expulsion from campus and a possible assault charge."

Glazy blue eyes blinked at him. Her double chins quivered. "Sorry. I'm just upset at being victimized twice. It's so unfair, especially since the stupid cops acted like I'm some nut case."

Marinde stepped out from behind the table. "Cora, I'm truly sorry about what's happened to you. May I get you some tea or more water?"

Cora sniffed and looked her up and down, as if to gauge her sincerity. "Tea would be nice, and maybe a donut. Make that two. I need comfort food."

Walter swooped in on Marinde. "Let me help you. You shouldn't have to carry all of that by yourself."

Evan spotted Janelle's frown. Jealousy? Or did she not want to be left alone to deal with customers?

Sydney joined her mother. "I'll do it, Mom. You've got more customers."

"Thanks." Marinde turned to Walter. "My daughter will help her, but I appreciate the offer."

Marinde's cheeks were colouring and she didn't meet his gaze. Evan couldn't tell if it was because she liked the guy or the exact opposite. Maybe she simply didn't want the attention. Marinde did seem shy and a bit introverted.

"No problem," Walter said. "Anytime."

Marinde returned to her table, while Sydney headed for the lobby. Mercifully, Cora also retreated to her display.

"You can go back to patrolling," Evan said to Felix. "Make sure you check all bathrooms at the end of each shift."

"Got it." Felix scurried off.

"Thanks, Evvy," Gran whispered. "But I doubt that was the demon's last word. The woman causes trouble every damn day."

As Gran left, Evan edged closer to Cora, although not too close. "May I ask you about the incident in the ladies' washroom yesterday?"

Once again, Cora's glassy blue eyes reminded Evan of his ex's satanic doll. Her mouth opened just like that damn doll used to. If she said *Mama* he'd scream.

"*Incident*? Is that what you call attempted murder?"

Evan gaped at her. Attempted murder? How was he supposed to respond to that? "I'm just trying to understand what happened."

Cora let out a huff of air. "Look, all I remember is a thwack between my shoulder blades that knocked the air out of me. I pitched forward and my forehead struck the edge of the sink." Cora pushed back the tuque to expose an angry red welt. "Then I fell backward and hit my head on the floor. It's a miracle I'm not dead!"

Evan scribbled in his notebook. "Just before you were pushed, did you glimpse someone in the mirror, by any chance?"

"No."

"You mentioned that you had sensitivities to scents. Did you recall any perfume or anything?"

"No!" Her hideous eyes flashed. "It all happened too fast."

Evan wasn't sure he wanted to ask the next question, but Okeyo would expect nothing less. "Aside from Flo, is there anyone else who would want to harm you?"

"There sure in hell is," Cora shot back. "You don't know half of what's going on around here, but I know plenty of secrets."

She leaned closer. "Sex secrets." A nasty smile spread across her face. "I could ruin marriages and reputations."

Evan thought about the blackmail angle. "Anyone's in particular?"

"Ask Martha and her buddies," Cora went on. "God knows they have a lot to answer for, and they aren't the only ones. It's about time the cheaters were held accountable. Mark my words, young man, someone's gonna pay."

She turned her attention to the customers ambling toward her table.

Evan headed toward the front of the gym, thinking that old people led spicier lives than he thought. He joined Sully and Sydney who'd stopped to gaze at the Christmas tree.

"Isn't it pretty?" Sydney remarked, her fingertip tracing an origami star. "Someone put a lot of work into the decorations."

"How's it going?" Evan asked.

Turning to him, Sydney smiled. "Good. You two chat. I'd better get Cora's food before she has a complete meltdown."

"I thought she already had," Evan replied.

"No." She gave him a look. "It can get

much worse, trust me."

As she left for the lobby, Sully said, "We're going out after the fair's over. Didn't even hesitate when I asked."

"Cool."

"Yep." He turned to Evan. "You look stressed. What's up?"

Evan told him about the mustard and alluded to Cora's secrets about the vendors. "I could use an extra pair of ears and eyes. If you hear any gossip about vendors hooking up, or rivalry, or other crap let me know."

"Sure, but don't believe half of what you hear, dude. Syd says that most of the vendors are needy, immature liars."

Evan couldn't discount all of the gossip, though. Janelle and Walter were a couple, and Agnes certainly didn't hide her interest in men. Did Cora know something about Agnes's love life? More to the point, what did Gran know, and how far would she go to protect her friends from embarrassment or humiliation?

Chapter Six

"Really, Evvy," Gran said, shifting in her chair. "I don't think we should discuss seniors' romantic lives at the dinner table. My, this chocolate cheesecake is delicious, don't you think?" She scraped the last bite onto her fork.

"No one's coming back to the table, Gran. Meal's over. This is the perfect time to talk."

Normally, Evan didn't eat with the family on Saturday nights, but he had questions for Gran and wanted to make sure that she couldn't avoid him.

"I should help your mother with the

dishes." Gran started to rise.

"I've got it, Mom," Evan's mother called out from the kitchen. "Stay there and talk to Evan."

Evan smiled at Gran's chagrinned face. He'd conspired with Mom earlier.

"As I said," Evan began, "I heard that the bad blood between Cora Riddell and others goes beyond knitting patterns and price slashing, and into romantic rivalry."

"Who told you that?"

"Cora."

"She's always spinning tales. It's her most effective way to cause trouble."

Evan kept his gaze fixed on her. "Based on what I've seen of Walter and the way he fawned over Marinde Marchant in front of Janelle, Cora's not exaggerating. So tell me what you know, and does it have anything to do with Agnes?"

Gran's wariness sharpened into suspicion. "What did that blabbermouth say about Agnes and Walter? It was just a short-lived fling anyway."

Evan gaped at her. "You mean they actually went out?"

Gran glanced at him, then focused on her cake. "Cora didn't tell you?"

"She said to ask you."

"Really, Evvy." Gran made a point of dabbing crumbs from the table cloth. "It's not right to talk about a best friend's personal life."

"Tell him, Mother."

Evan smiled when Mom appeared in the doorway, wiping her hands on a tea towel. She was short like Gran but slimmer. Truth was, those two were far too much alike. Both said what they thought and played by their own rules when it suited them.

Mom swept strands of dark blonde hair from her face as she turned to Evan. "Agnes dated Walter for about a month. She was really ticked when he dumped her."

Gran's mouth dropped open. "You've been eavesdropping!"

"How else am I going to know what kind of disaster you're getting into?"

Evan propped his elbows on the table and slid his hand under his chin. He'd heard this argument before. One of the reasons Gran had moved in with them was so Mom could keep a closer eye on her mischief-making mother. Gran cooked up more dumb schemes than people half her age.

"Walter was seeing other women while

going out with Agnes," Mom told him.

Evan's eyebrows rose as he turned to Gran. "Who?"

Gran's pinched mouth relaxed just enough to mutter, "Cora, for one."

"You're joking."

"Technically, Walter never took her out. He just ate supper at her place a couple of times, but I suspect that Cora offered more than food. That dog wouldn't turn down any offer."

Mom shook her head and retreated to the kitchen.

"I hear that he gets his sex pills from some cheap place in Mexico." Gran sipped her tea, then dabbed the corner of her mouth with a napkin. "Do you have any idea how much that stuff costs up here?"

"No." Evan hoped to god he'd never need to find out. "Focus, Gran. Please. This is important."

She huffed. "Walter was seeing Cora, but then he took up with Agnes. After that Janelle came into the picture."

"He was seeing all three women at once?" Evan asked.

"Yep."

"Quite the player."

"If you say so," she said, her expression filled with disdain. "Anyway, somehow Cora found out about Janelle and told Agnes. Everyone knows that Cora was and still is jealous of both women."

"How did Agnes react?"

"She was furious," his mom called out from the kitchen.

"Thank you, Miss Blabbermouth!" Gran yelled.

"You're welcome!"

"Maybe Agnes did follow Cora down the back hallway," Evan said, "intending to confront her about something, only things got out of hand."

"No, Evvy. I told you, Agnes wasn't anywhere near that hallway."

"I heard otherwise."

Gran leaned forward. "Who said that?"

"I can't reveal sources."

She studied him, then gave a satisfied smirk. "Bet it was Janelle. She sure didn't want Walter to keep seeing Agnes and Cora. And she knows that Walter still has a soft spot for Agnes. Probably worries that he'll take up with her again. She'd hate that. Janelle always needs a man in her life."

"Now who's spreading gossip?" Mom

called out.

"It's not gossip if it's true," Gran insisted, and leaned forward. "Listen to me, Janelle is nobody's friend, she just pretends she is. The woman plays head games, which is why people didn't want her organizing the fair anymore. She had her favourites too, ya know. Anyhow, she and Walter won't last, seeing as how she's married and worried about her kids finding out."

Evan sat back in his chair. "Aren't old people supposed to have higher standards and lead less sordid lives?"

"What you don't know about life, Evvy..." Gran clicked her tongue. "Janelle's husband has ALS and lives in a care home. She hasn't had a true companion for some time, and as I said, she's needy in just about every way imaginable."

Janelle did a good job of hiding it, Evan thought. "Do her kids live with her?"

"No, they're grown up and living in other parts of the country. But I hear they're coming home for Christmas." Gran glanced toward the kitchen. "Grown children can be pretty damn judgemental when it comes to their parents' desire to lead an active life."

"I heard that," Mom said.

Gran muttered something Evan didn't quite catch and probably wouldn't want to.

"Flo implied that Cora wasn't above blackmailing people," he said. "Could she be doing that to Janelle?"

"If Cora's that desperate for cash, then it's possible. But that's a dangerous game that could backfire, if it hasn't already." Gran gave him a meaningful look. "What if Janelle tried to hurt her?"

"There's no proof yet, and I sure hope you'll keep that thought to yourself."

Gran shook her head. "Romantic rivalry and grudges won't matter soon because of the other reason Walter and Janelle won't last."

"Which is?"

"He has no intention of hitching his wagon to any woman. You have to understand, Evvy. Most of our seniors are broke and looking for someone to take care of them emotionally and financially. Walter has a lot of money that he doesn't intend to share. As far as I'm concerned, he exploits lonely, desperate women."

"Which might result in a few grudges," Evan replied.

Was Agnes one of those who held a

grudge? Not that Gran would admit anything. But Evan had noticed that Flo and Agnes ate here a lot. And Agnes moved into Flo's two-bedroom condo a couple months back to share expenses. Last week Mom commented on how she felt sorry for seniors who had to resort to food banks. Were Flo and Agnes that destitute?

Evan's phone rang. Oh, no. It was the shift supervisor, Zach. Supervisors only called him when there was a problem they couldn't deal with or something serious had gone down.

"What's going on, Zach?"

"There's been more vandalism in the gym. Someone gouged a few wooden bowls on a table at the back of the room."

Evan sat upright. "Gouged?"

"Yeah. Too wide and deep to have been done with an ordinary knife or scissors," Zach replied. "I'm thinking someone got hold of the missing hatchet you told us about."

"Shit. So someone's walking around campus, destroying vendors' work with STT's property?" Property that he and Steve had left out in the open. Double shit. Evan had talked to every guard and facilities staff who'd worked this weekend, and no one had picked up the hatchet.

"At least only one table was damaged," Zach said. "We checked."

"Okay." Still, this was a nightmare. Evan noticed Gran's expression turning to stone.

"How the hell did the suspect get in?"

"We found a bit of folded paper lodged in the back door lock to prevent it from latching properly."

"Terrific." Evan sighed. "I guess the camera's probably been on the parking lot and not the far side of the building?"

"Yep, but maybe we'll see the suspect getting in and out of a car. I haven't had time to review the footage, but I will soon." Zach paused. "Can you ask your grandmother to let the vendor know?"

"Sure. Take photos and write a report, then email it to Okeyo and me. Make sure the building's closely monitored inside and out, and keep looking for the damn hatchet!"

"Ten-four."

As Evan hung up, Gran's pensive expression became fearful. "Who do I need to call?"

"Walter. His bowls have been slashed."

He told her about the missing hatchet.

"Well, crap my pants and call me stupid," she said. "You could be onto something about a grudge, and let me tell ya, Walter won't take it well. He's proud of his bowls."

"Are there any other suspects besides Agnes and Cora?"

Gran stared at what remained of her dessert. "Maybe Janelle, if she thinks she's about to get dumped. And I don't believe for one minute that Agnes would do something like that."

Evan sighed. "I guess that puts Cora at the top of the list."

"Totally. She was seriously pissed at being dumped, although she knows what Walter's like and should have seen it coming. Can't imagine her being that good in bed either."

"Mother!" Mom yelled from the kitchen.

"I'm entitled to my opinion!"

Evan shook his head at this totally gross turn in the conversation. He wished he'd had time to review all of the CCTV footage from Friday afternoon. He'd make it a priority tomorrow.

"Maybe I should do a little investigating

on my own," Gran said.

Was she freaking kidding? "Absolutely not."

"I know these people, Evvy. They'll talk to me. Maybe I'll learn something useful."

"If you approach the guilty party and ask the wrong questions, he or she may go after you."

"We *have* to do something, because I have another theory about why all this is happening, and it's more worrisome than Walter's conquests." Gran leaned closer to him, her expression tense. "What if all this destruction is about ruining my reputation as the fair's organizer?"

Evan sat back in his chair. Maybe she had a point. "I need to ask you something." The trepidation on Gran's face didn't deter him. "This morning, Agnes said that your ability to organize the fair will be questioned again. Aside from Janelle, has anyone else been doing that?"

Gran fiddled with her fork. "A handful of vendors didn't want Janelle to resign. Truth is, she wants to control the fair again, but not in an official capacity that subjects her to criticism. Janelle wants someone in charge whom she can control." Gran gave him a long look. "She could have stepped up her mission to cause trouble, hoping that I'll either quit or be forced out. That's why we have to work together to solve this mess."

"Let security handle this, Gran. We'll figure this out, I promise."

He had to. If Walter got the police involved about his bowls, Okeyo would be pissed. If Evan wanted to keep his reputation and improve his chance of joining the RCMP, then he'd have to come up with answers tomorrow.

"I'm going to need a list of Janelle's friends," he said to Gran.

"Sure." She smiled sweetly. "Whatever you say."

Uh-oh. Harsh experience had proven that whenever Gran smiled and vowed cooperation, a disaster of epic proportion was bound to follow.

Chapter Seven

Slouched in his office chair, Evan slurped his second mug of coffee this morning. He despised 7:00 a.m. starts on Sundays, but at least the craft fair ended today and he'd have tomorrow off. He'd also be driving Cecelia to the airport.

When he drove up this morning, Walter and Janelle were already waiting by the doors. Walter was so pissed about the damage to his bowls that he simply wanted to pack up his things and go home. Gran had assured Evan that Walter hadn't mentioned calling the cops, but this didn't mean he wouldn't.

Cora Riddell showed up early as well. The surprise on her face when she saw the damaged bowls seemed genuine.

"Not much fun being on the receiving end of a hate crime, is it?" she'd remarked with a vindictive smile. "Some people have it coming, though, given the shitty way they treat others."

At that point, Janelle shouted, "Mind your own business, you twisted old hag!"

Cora was so stunned by the rebuke that she'd retreated to her own table without another word. Evan was equally shocked. Sure, everyone lost it now and then, but just how nasty was Janelle's dark side? Had she lied about Agnes following Cora down that hall simply to cause trouble?

"You gonna call the cops about all this vandalism?" Cora had asked Evan. "They can't be as inept as you security people."

There'd been no point arguing with the woman, so he ignored her.

The ringing landline startled him. Evan picked it up, and cringed again at the sound of Okeyo's voice. "I read Zach's incident report and saw the photos. The vendor must be pretty angry."

"Yeah. He packed his things and left

without saying a word."

Evan had phoned Okeyo last night to tell him about the vandalism. The big guy insisted on reading a thorough incident report first before deciding whether to involve the police. Evan had hoped not to worry him about the missing hatchet, but there'd been no choice. Okeyo hadn't been happy to hear that Evan forgot to put it in the security vehicle, or that he hadn't notified Okeyo earlier.

"Insurance notwithstanding, this makes us look bad, Evan. I'll have to call the cops, but it would help if we identified the culprit first. Which reminds me, did you review Steve's notebook?"

"Yes, and nothing shows any time lapse in patrols, unless he deliberately wrote down the wrong times. I called Steve and he swears he had nothing to do with the elf/Santa display." Evan didn't add that the guy had been pissed about being questioned. "I still have to review CCTV footage of the comings and goings at the front entrance and parking lot last night. Maybe something will show up."

"If you find anything, call me, and we'll see where we go from there. And get it done fast, Evan. I'm counting on you."

"Will do."

He clicked on the camera footage that Zach had bookmarked. At 6:45 p.m., a silver compact pulled right up to the gym, on the far side. A short individual in a dark parka with a scarf wrapped around his or her face stepped out of the vehicle. The person—likely a woman—disappeared down the side of the building where the back entrance was located. She returned ten minutes later.

Evan froze the footage. The parka looked bulky and she was hugging herself. The hatchet wasn't overly long. What if the suspect still possessed the hatchet? Did she intend to cause more damage today? But how? Since the gym was again packed with customers, how could an act of vandalism go unnoticed?

"Alpha Three to Alpha One?"

Evan groaned at the sound of Felix's edgy tone. "Go ahead."

"Can you come to the gym right away? There's a problem."

"What sort of problem?"

"Cora Riddell's about to throw a chair at your grandma."

Evan heard shouts in the background.

Terrific. If that woman kept antagonizing people, someone really would kill her. "On my way."

Two minutes later he pulled up to the building, then jogged inside. Squeezing between a senior with a walker and the Christmas tree, he spotted Cecelia.

"Oh! I was about to pick up another little gift for you," she said, "but I don't want you to see it."

"Oh. Wow." Was he supposed to do that too? "I won't look." Man, he'd forgotten to pick up the necklace and earrings set. "Sorry, hon, I've got to go," he blurted. "Gran's having problems with one of the vendors."

"I thought I heard raised voices." She strained for a better look at the source. "What's the issue?"

"I'm about to find out."

Working his way to the back of the room, Evan spotted Cora gripping a fold-up chair. God, she really did look crazy. Her gaze darted everywhere and sweat trickled down her temples.

"I am *not* leaving!" Cora screeched over the shoppers' chatter. "You can't make me!"

"I heard you threaten Flo, which violates

the fair's rules," Gran replied, hands on hips, chin jutting out. "Pack up and leave, or I'll have my grandson escort you out of here."

Evan winced. Activity in the immediate vicinity of the pair had ceased. Marinde and the vendor beside her were talking and nodding toward the two combatants.

"Flo threatened me first," Cora retorted. "Bet you won't throw her out!"

"I also heard you say that someone should destroy the rest of her things. That's unacceptable."

Felix rushed up to Evan. "The redhead's totally freaking out. It's almost as if she's tweaking on something. If they gave her medication at the hospital, maybe she's having a bad reaction."

Evan stepped up to her. "Mrs. Riddell, are you all right?"

"Tell your granny to back off!" Spittle appeared at the corners of Cora's mouth, and there was something weird with her eyes. They seemed darker than usual.

"Why should I?" Gran replied. "You've been badmouthing vendors all day. I've worked hard to create a positive environment, Cora, and you're ruining everything!"

Felix was right. Cora's problem could be medical. Evan radioed Gus, asking him to come to the gym. "The patient from Friday is here, and I think something's wrong with her." Evan described what he was seeing.

"Be there shortly," Gus answered. "I'm with the bike patroller. She just took a spill and won't be riding anymore today."

"I heard." Evan had asked dispatch to find a replacement. "Come as soon as you can."

"Roger that."

"No one's kicking me out of here!" Cora lifted the chair.

Oh, hell. She wasn't going to throw it, was she? Wrestling the chair from an old lady would make him look like a bullying moron. If she didn't calm down, though, he'd have to take it from her.

"Now, Cora," Marinde said from behind the table. "You won't attract customers that way. You're sabotaging your own sales."

"But I need to p-protect myself!" Cora lowered the chair and looked up at the ceiling. "Oh! I see glittery b-birds!"

Evan heard the gasps. He looked up. Nothing. Was hallucinating a side effect of the concussion or a bad drug reaction?

"Stop it, Cora!" Gran said. "You're scaring everybody."

Cora's stare remained fixed on the ceiling. She started swaying.

"Mrs. Riddell," Evan said, moving closer. "Please put the chair down. I don't want anyone getting hurt."

As she blinked at Evan, he realized that her pupils were dilated. Shit. "Mrs. Riddell?"

"The glitter's falling!" Cora stepped back. "I'm gonna die!"

Evan wished to hell that Gus got here fast.

"Fire!" someone yelled from the other end of the gym. "The tree's on fire!"

Evan and Gran gaped at each other in horror.

Chapter Eight

Evan ran as he shouted to Felix, "Get the fire extinguisher! Excuse me, folks! Coming through!"

"I have one at the registration table!" Gran exclaimed, running toward the lobby.

As people scattered, Evan spotted small flames at the back of the tree. Damn it! He'd hoped there'd been a mistake. "All units, code red in the gym! Code red!" He turned to the shoppers. "Everyone, please leave the gym immediately by using the back exit!" Customers and vendors stared, but only a few made an effort to move. "Please!" he yelled louder. "The place could fill with smoke!"

"Evan?" Cecelia called anxiously from the next aisle over.

"Help get the seniors outside!"

Sully appeared beside him. "What's going on?"

"Just another freakin' day at the craft fair. Everyone out!" he shouted. "*Now*, please!"

"I'd better see if Sydney's all right," Sully said.

"Help!" Cora screamed. "I'm smothered in glitter! They're crapping all over me. I can't b-breathe!"

Evan glanced over his shoulder, dismayed to see that she'd made her way toward the front of the gym.

Sweating profusely, her face twisted in horror, Cora put her hands over her head and ducked. "Aagh!" At that point, Cora's eyes rolled upward and she slumped to the floor.

"Shit!" Evan ran up to her. "Mrs. Riddell?"

Cecelia joined him and checked Cora's pulse. Her first-aid skills had come in handy more than once. Evan radioed dispatch and requested an ambulance, then asked Gus to join him ASAP.

"Can you handle this while I deal with the tree?" he asked Cecelia. "Gus is on his way."

"Sure," she answered. "Go!"

Evan raced up to Felix, who was behind the tree with the fire extinguisher, spewing chemicals everywhere. Customers and vendors stayed well back.

"Okay, buddy. Stop!" Evan touched Felix's bony shoulder. "Fire's out."

Steve entered the gym and gaped at the mess. "Figures."

Evan sighed. "What are you doing here?"

"Dispatch called me in, and since I couldn't sleep anyway..." He shrugged and stared at the dripping tree. "Another clusterfuck on your watch, huh, Evan? Congrats."

"Everyone get back right now!" Gran yelled through the megaphone.

Evan winced. "Thanks, Gran. I think they've figured it out."

"You should have told them to leave," Steve remarked.

"I have, but these people don't listen."

"It was just a tiny fire, Evvy. No alarm even went off," Gran said. "And you'll never get anyone to leave now that the crisis is over."

Didn't she understand that he wanted to avoid another one? If someone was determined to sabotage the fair, then they'd just raised the bar big time.

Evan's radio crackled as the rest of the team reported in, as was proper procedure. At least they'd followed protocol. One guard was monitoring signals and digital messages at the main fire panel. The other was watching the panel in the basement of this building. Both guards reported that no alarms were showing up.

"Okay, thanks," Evan said.

"This is horrible," Gran mumbled, studying the tree. "Our beautiful decorations are ruined."

"Go get the cones and tape from the security vehicle," Evan said, tossing Steve the keys. "We need to cordon off the area."

Muttering under his breath, Steve stormed out of the gym as Gus came in.

He stared at the chemically-coated tree. "Should I even ask?"

"No," Evan answered.

Gus scanned the room. "Where's the patient?"

"On the floor, two rows over." Evan pointed in the general direction. "My girlfriend's with her. She's a nursing student."

"What patient?" Gran asked. "What happened?"

"Cora Riddell collapsed."

"Can't say I'm surprised, seeing as how she was working herself into a frenzy." Gran shook her head. "Woman's crazy."

Evan turned to Gus. "I think she was hallucinating. Claimed to see birds and was going on about how they were crapping glitter on her. I think she was referring to the origami birds on the Christmas tree."

"Is she on medication?" Gus asked.

"Not that I know of," Gran answered. "But she could have been prescribed something at the hospital."

Four firefighters entered the gym and surveyed the damage. Evan knew they'd show up. The moment he'd called the code red, protocol required that dispatch contact the fire department.

"Felix, can you show Gus where Cora is?"

"Sure."

Gran hurried after them just as Steve

returned with the cones and tape.

The older firefighter zeroed in on Evan. "Who's in charge here?"

"That guy." Steve nodded toward Evan. "For now."

Asshole. After Evan introduced himself, he said, "Fire's out. No one's been hurt."

"Why didn't you evacuate the building?" the older firefighter asked.

"Told ya," Steve remarked.

Evan glared at him. "Can you get a couple of mops and a pail of water? You and Felix will need to clean up the mess."

Muttering something inaudible, Steve marched out of the room.

"I told people to leave more than once," Evan explained to the firefighter, "but most of them refused, probably because it was out quickly and there was no alarm."

Scepticism deepened the lines on the firefighter's face. "Are you sure the alarms are working properly?"

"They're tested every month."

"We'll check them anyway." The firefighter nodded toward the vendors. "If the flames had jumped to some of those tables, you people would have had a big problem."

Evan hated having to defend himself. "Believe me, if the situation hadn't been contained right away, I would have dragged the shoppers out. But as you can see, this is primarily a seniors' event. Many use canes and walkers, so making them rush out of here could have caused falls and broken bones."

As the older firefighter studied the spectators, understanding dawned on his face. "Any idea how the fire started?"

"None."

Felix rejoined them, still carrying the fire extinguisher. He wiped perspiration from beneath his blue bangs. "What a weekend."

Evan cringed. He didn't want outsiders to know about all the other shit that had happened.

Two paramedics entered the gym. "We had a report that a woman collapsed?"

"Yes, the first-aid attendant's with her." Evan turned to Felix. "Show them the way, then help Steve clean up."

"Don't do that yet." The older firefighter raised his hand. "We need a closer look." He turned to Evan. "I thought you said there were no injuries."

"Separate incident," Evan replied.

The firefighter gaped at him. "Is this a normal day for you?"

Evan sighed. "For this event, yeah." The fair would be over in about three hours. It couldn't end soon enough.

Gran returned, looking a little shaky. "Cora's semi-conscious and mumbling complete nonsense, but the first-aid guy thinks she'll be okay."

Evan's relief was short-lived. If someone had wanted to kill Cora, the culprit wouldn't be happy that she'd survived. Still, what if the plan was merely to shake her up? Use her as a distraction while the perp started the fire?

"Let's examine the tree," the firefighter said to his colleagues.

The crew unplugged the two cords of lights, then lowered the tree onto the tarp.

"Step back, people!" Gran yelled into the megaphone. "The fire department needs space!"

Evan was fairly certain that everyone had figured that much out, though a couple of seniors looked confused, not to mention a little startled by her outburst.

"Look at this," one of the younger

firefighters said as he showed them a charred box and two tea candles. "Two more boxes and another four candles fell out of the tree."

The older firefighter looked from Evan to Gran. "Don't tell me you people were using candles."

"Of course not," she answered. "That's ridiculous!"

"I think the candles were in the boxes," the younger firefighter said. "There's melted wax at the bottom, maybe to hold them in place."

Evan's spirits sank. "Arson?"

"Could be," the older firefighter responded. "Have you been having trouble with anyone at this event?"

Evan cleared his throat. "There's been a couple of incidents concerning the woman that the paramedics are with now. But I can confirm that she's been nowhere near the tree for the last twenty minutes."

The firefighter walked toward the nearest vendors. "Did any of you see someone hovering behind the tree?"

Everyone shook their heads.

Gran's fearful eyes glanced at Evan, then quickly turned away.

"Gran?" Evan asked. "What is it?"

"Nothing."

Gran couldn't meet his gaze. Evan suspected she didn't want to talk in front of the firefighters. Had she seen something?

"Cora's stabilized," Gus said as he approached Evan. "It looks like she ingested a hallucinogenic."

"You can't be serious!" Gran said. "Cora Riddell may be a lot of things but she's no drug user."

"Could someone have spiked whatever she was eating or drinking?" Gus asked.

Evan and Gran looked at each other.

"The blue bottle!" Grant blurted. "She's constantly drinking from it. You'd think she would have noticed something funny about the taste, though."

"Maybe the hallucinogen has no taste," Gus replied.

"Can one of you get a box to store this evidence in?" the younger firefighter asked.

"No problem," Gran replied, and hurried off.

"I'll get the bottle," Evan said.

He hadn't gone far when Cecelia intercepted him. "Where are you rushing off to?"

"To get Cora's water bottle. We think someone spiked it."

"Makes sense. I heard the paramedics talking, and I know a little about drugs. LSD is one that can be taken in liquid form. Just a few drops could do damage, although everyone responds differently."

"Does it have any taste?"

"Not as far as I know."

Evan reached the back of the room, surprised to find Marinde Marchant behind Cora's table, showing a baby blanket to a customer. Spotting the water, Evan pulled out a pair of latex gloves from the pouch on his equipment belt. Removing a plastic bag from a second pouch, he carefully lifted the bottle.

It felt light. Evan swished it around. Empty. Had Cora gulped every drop or had the culprit dumped the contents? Everyone would have been so focused on Cora's bizarre behaviour that the culprit could have dumped the evidence in the bathroom without being noticed. Out the corner of his eye, Evan saw Sully amble toward him.

"What are you doing?" Sully asked.

"Gathering evidence." Evan placed the bottle in the bag, then looked at the frowning Sully. "You look stressed. What's up?"

"Nothing. It's just chaotic in here." He glanced back at Sydney, who was busy helping customers.

"Did you seen anyone touch this water bottle?" Evan asked.

"Nope. I've only been here about five minutes, trying to help Sydney wrap soaps while her mom sells Mrs. Riddell's stuff for her. Maybe you can ask your grandmother to take over. I'm useless when it comes to wrapping and processing credit cards on phones."

Judging from Sydney's flustered gestures and haggard expression, she looked like she needed assistance.

"I can help out till Martha gets here," Cecelia offered.

"Would you?" Sully's face brightened. "That'd be awesome."

"Thanks, gorgeous." Evan squeezed her hand. "I've got to see about getting this bottle analyzed."

Cora was now on a gurney that the paramedics were maneuvering toward the lobby. Evan hurried up to them.

"I think this bottle was spiked with the

drug that the patient ingested. Maybe someone at the hospital can analyze it?"

"It needs to go to the police first," the paramedic replied.

The older firefighter appeared, carrying a cardboard box. "Here's your evidence and make sure no one else touches it." He handed Evan the box. "Your guards told us about the vandalism incidents. Looks like you've got a serious problem. Good thing we called the cops."

Oh, shit. Evan stared at the man. "That was my supervisor's call to make."

"Not anymore, son. Since this could be arson, we've contacted the police. Normally, they wouldn't pay too much attention to a dumb prank that didn't harm anyone. But given the vandalism and the patient with the paramedics, they might look at things differently." He gave Evan a half-assed grin. "Relax, son. They know the fire was small and things are under control, so it's not like they'll be racing over here with sirens blaring."

Still, he didn't like it. A police presence would upset Gran and Okeyo. And how the hell was he supposed to solve this freakin' crime wave over the next few minutes?

Okay. Time to think like a cop and figure out the next logical step.

"Steve, Felix," he called. "Take photos and write detailed notes about everything you've done from the time you arrived until now."

As they pulled out their phones, two elderly women, one with a walker, the other with a cane, were chatting as they entered the gym. They were so focused on their conversation that they bumped into a cone and nearly hit Felix.

"Ma'am?" one of the firefighters called out, then maneuvered them away from the area.

The older firefighter scratched the side of his face as he looked at Evan. "Normally, we leave things as we find them for the police, but under the circumstances, we'll move the tree and tarp outside, but one of your guards should watch the evidence until the police show up. And lock up those candles. No one should touch anything until they arrive. We'll also need to examine the annunciator panel and alarms."

"Felix, escort the firefighters to each building when they're ready." He turned to Steve. "Once the tarp is moved, make sure the floor's clean and dry, then watch over the tree and tarp until the police arrive."

As Steve muttered something under his breath, two of the firefighters lifted the tree while the other two carefully picked up the tarp. Felix gave them a hand, but Steve just stood there, arms crossed and watching. Evan shook his head until he spotted a depressed-looking Sully among the spectators. Maybe Sydney was annoyed with him for not being more helpful. He would have asked if everything was okay, but he needed to talk to Gran.

Still carrying the box, Evan hurried up to her and said, "Cecelia's looking after Cora's table 'cause she still has customers. But she needs to get back to studying."

She was about to answer when Janelle approached. "Agnes needs your help at registration, Martha. She's dropping coins everywhere and seems frazzled."

Evan thought Janelle had left with Walter this morning, but apparently she had come back. Did she want to see if other problems cropped up? He didn't like the smug, barely concealed smile on Janelle's face.

Gran's gaze bore into her. "Maybe you

could help out by taking over for the young lady who volunteered to watch Cora's table."

Janelle's smile vanished. "Wouldn't it be best to simply pack it up? She wouldn't want us touching her products."

"She'd forgive us if we sold a few things."

Janelle shook her head. "I don't know about that. Cora was more volatile than usual this morning, and acting very strange."

Evan didn't recall seeing her when Gran and Cora were arguing. How long had Janelle been at the fair and what had she been doing? More to the point, had anyone seen her near the Christmas tree?

"Are you going to pitch in, Janelle?" Gran asked. "Or are you just gonna keep criticizing from the cheap seats?"

Janelle's head snapped back, as if she'd been slapped. "I will *not* be spoken to that way, Martha."

"Then maybe you should bloody well leave."

Janelle smacked the tip of her cane on the floor. She gripped the handle so tightly that her knuckles turned white. "Fine. I'll work her table, but don't say I never do anything for you."

As Janelle made her way down the aisle, Gran swore under her breath. "I don't know who I despise more, her or Cora."

"Think she had anything to do with all the trouble?" Evan asked quietly.

Gran's glowering stare looked about ready to burn a hole in Janelle's receding back.

"Not really, no. But I do think she's having a hell of a good time witnessing the disasters." She turned to Evan. "Earlier, you said something about reviewing the camera footage from Friday. Have you had a chance to do that?"

"I started to, but didn't finish." He paused. "Why? Is there someone you think I'll see?"

"Maybe. I'll let you know after you've taken a look at everything."

"Evan!" Steve's voice rose above the din. "I'm due for a break. You going to stay here until the cops arrive or what?"

Asshole. Did he have to say it so loudly?

"I've got to bring this box to Okeyo, but I'll have Felix cover for you as soon as he's back."

Gran's mouth fell open. "What do you

mean, the cops are on their way?"

Oops. "Sorry, Gran, but the fire department called them."

Gran ushered him into the lobby. "Evvy, we've got another three hours before the fair ends," she whispered. "What if the saboteur is planning a big finale? She needs to be stopped, fast!"

"She?" Evan saw the same fearful expression when the firefighters showed them the charred gift boxes and candles. "Why do I get the feeling that you know who the suspect is?"

She inhaled deeply and peered up at him. "I can't prove anything."

"If you give me a name, maybe I can. I don't want to wait until I've reviewed all the footage."

Gran clutched his hand. "If I'm wrong, my credibility will be ruined and I won't be allowed to run anything, and I really like this job, Evvy. It gets me out of bed in the morning."

"If this person is guilty, then I'm sure that proof will be found. I'm guessing there'll be prints all over the water bottle and maybe on the candles." Evan tucked the box of evidence under his arm. "So, who are we talking about?"

Gran looked around, moved even closer to Evan, and whispered, "Marinde Marchant."

Chapter Nine

Evan stared through the security vehicle's rain-splattered windshield. Sitting here with the engine off and the blurry view of buildings suited him just fine. He'd seen enough shit this weekend. Right now, he needed solitude to write detailed notes about this morning's debacle.

"Let's be clear, Evvy," Gran had said. "I didn't see Marinde near the tree, but I did see her twisting the lid off of Cora's water bottle and peering inside, like she knew there was something wrong with it. But then she got distracted with customers, and I went about my business."

Gran's theory made sense. Marinde was short. She could have been the one entering the building Saturday night. Was she also the one who'd stayed behind late Friday afternoon to squirt mustard over two tables? Sydney had told him that she saw Agnes head down the hall after Cora, but what if she'd lied to protect her mother? Was she part of this?

Felix contacted him over the radio. "The fire department just left. "There's no problem with the panel or alarms. I think some of them might stay behind and wait for the cops, but I don't know."

Evan didn't know what their protocol was. Right now, he didn't care.

"Okay, good. Steve needs to go on a break, so stay in the gym until closing time. I'll join you as soon as I can." Given Felix's excitability and Steve's laziness, neither would be a good candidate to observe the Marchants. He'd have to do it himself, but first he needed to brief Okeyo and finish reviewing Friday's CCTV footage after the fair closed.

A sudden rap on Evan's window made him flinch. It was Sully, one of the few people he didn't mind seeing at this moment. He'd meant to talk to him in the gym, but there'd been too damn much going on.

Evan rolled the window down. "Get in."

As Sully did so he said, "Sydney's too busy to go for lunch. Any leads on who caused the fire?"

"No." Evan watched him. "What do Sydney and her mom say about it?

"They've haven't talked much." He glanced at Evan. "What about you? Any theories?"

Evan didn't want to lie, but given Sully's feelings for Sydney, he had to be careful. "No, and I could use help to make sure nothing else happens before the fair ends."

Sully looked out the side window. "I might not hang around."

Why not? Did you and Sydney have a fight?"

Sully shook his head. "I just…well, I feel bad for her, ya know? She takes a lot of crap from everyone."

"Does that include her mom?"

Sully shrugged and kept his gaze on the window.

Evan tried not to appear too interested.

"Marinde seems cool. Not the bossy type."

"She's passive-aggressive bossy. Asks Syd to do stuff in a polite way, but then works her hard. Doesn't even like her taking coffee breaks." He paused. "I think Marinde resents me hanging around."

"How does Sydney feel about that?"

"She's pissed, but Syd also feels sorry for her. Marinde's taken a lot of bullshit from that freak show, Cora Riddell. Syd's tried to get their table moved, but no one listens." Sully gave him a long look. "Especially your grandma."

Evan nodded. "Sorry about that. I'll see if I can persuade her to do things differently next time."

Sully's stomach grumbled. "I need a donut."

Sully always ate donuts when he was under stress. Usually, he brought two-day-old baked goods from his father's bakery, but he probably hadn't expected this day to go so badly.

"They're selling donuts in the gym lobby," Evan said. "I'll drive you there." He kept meaning to question the food volunteers, but they were always rushing about.

On the short ride over, Sully's glum expression remained fixed. If Sydney's mother really didn't like him then that could explain his mood. But what if Sully saw Marinde doing something she shouldn't have?

"Sully, did you see anyone near Cora's blue water bottle this morning?"

Sully flinched. "What? No! Why would you say that?"

He'd seen something all right. "Just curious."

Evan parked, then headed up the steps. The damaged tree and tarp were off to the side, protected by the overhang and the recycling bins placed in front to keep people from getting too close. Felix stood nearby, apparently, still covering for Steve. He paced back and forth, looking cold.

"If you can see the tarp and tree from the window in the door," Evan said, "then you might as well stay inside."

"Thanks."

The main entrance to the gym was propped open. Evan didn't need to be told why. Smells from the torched tree still lingered. For once, there were only a couple of customers at the registration desk, and two more at the food table.

While Sully ordered food, Evan headed for the condiments table. The little table had been pushed against the wall separating the gym from the lobby. Two of the plastic yellow, red, and green bottles were on their sides, adding to the drips and smears marking the plastic table cloth.

Evan strolled toward a poodle-haired woman stirring a pot of boiled wieners on the portable stove. The name tag pinned to her apron said *Edna*. "Excuse me, Edna. Can you tell me if any of the mustard bottles were missing when you came in yesterday morning?"

She peered at him through large, square eyeglasses. "You're wondering if someone used one of ours to destroy Flo and Cora's work. So were we. I'm surprised you didn't ask earlier."

Evan bit back his irritation. "I saw how busy you've been."

"Uh-huh." She continued peering at him. "The mustard wasn't missing, but it was out of place. I always make sure they're lined up properly before I leave for the night. Mustard, ketchup, then relish. But the mustard was off to the side, near the edge of the table. It was also lighter, and I should know because I filled it the night before. Had to refill it again yesterday morning."

Evan glanced at Sully as he showed Edna a receipt for his purchase. "I guess you didn't see anyone hanging near the condiments table at the end of the fair?"

"No, there was too much cleaning up to do." Using tongs, she lifted a wiener from the pot and plunked it in the bun. "Lots of people walked past that table on their way the washrooms." Edna handed Sully a hot dog, which he juggled with two donuts and a can of pop.

"Gotta go," Sully said, his face now flushed. "Just remembered that I have chores at home."

"You coming back later?"

Sully barely met his gaze. "Dunno." He hurried out of the lobby.

"Your friend's really taken with Sydney Marchant," Edna said. "I saw him waiting for her after the fair on Friday, though Marinde didn't seem to appreciate him being there."

"She said so?"

"Not to me." Edna paused. "I went to pour the wiener water down the toilet and ran into Marinde and Sydney in the bathroom. Marinde was telling her daughter that the boy was a waste of time. They stopped talking when they saw me, but Sydney sure looked angry."

"What time would that have been?"

"I'd say between four-fifteen and four-thirty." Edna shook her head. "It's really too bad to see them fighting after all they've been through. I suspect that Marinde's a tad overprotective."

"I take it they've had some tough times?"

Edna's expression became pensive. "I'm not one to gossip, mind you."

Seriously? Evan struggled to keep his facial muscles from twitching. "It's just that maybe I can help Sully understand Mrs. Marchant a little better if he knows where she's coming from."

The old gal studied Evan, then glanced around the room. She leaned over the table and whispered, "Marinde's been in an emotionally abusive marriage for years. I think her husband hits her. Based on what I've seen, the creep has no respect for his wife or his daughter."

"Sydney's been abused too?"

"I think so. Marinde knows that poor girl deserves better. She's been working lots of craft fairs to earn enough cash to leave him. It's finally happening right after Christmas. She and Sydney are moving back east, but you'd best keep that to yourself."

"Okay." Evan wondered if Sydney had confided this to Sully. "Does Sydney want to go away?"

"Up until this weekend, I would have said yes. But she seems quite taken with your friend. He might be the first boy who's shown an interest in her." Edna paused. "Sydney's only eighteen and doesn't have a job. Her options are limited."

"Think she'll stand up to her mother if she really wants to stay?"

"If she's been trying, I doubt she'll succeed," Edna replied. "Beneath Marinde Marchant's mousy exterior is an iron will. She's been working on her exit strategy with single-minded determination for five years. She's not about to give up now and I can't picture her leaving Sydney behind."

A customer approached Edna, so Evan stepped away. If this was Marinde's last fair, she might use the opportunity to let Gran—and a few others—know exactly what she thought of them. Marinde could have grabbed the mustard bottle on her way out of the bathroom, then waited until everyone had gone before she returned to the gym and got to work.

Angry Santa didn't seem like the type of stunt she'd pull, though. On the other hand, Evan didn't know the woman. As for Walter and his damaged bowls, given the abuse Marinde was suffering from one man, the attention of a horn dog like Walter might not have been welcome.

"Hey, darling." Cecelia was suddenly beside him, slipping her arm through his. "I sold a few things for Cora. The woman with the cane took over for me."

"Good." Evan surveyed the customers leaving the gym with overflowing bags. Despite everything, it looked like the fair was a success." He turned to Cecelia. "You've been chatting with a lot of vendors. Any idea what they think about all the trouble?"

"It depends on who you talk to," Cecelia replied. "Some feel that the incidents have ruined the fair's reputation and cost them sales. Others are amused by everything and think it'll give customers the incentive to come back next year just to see what happens next."

Evan rolled his eyes. No way would it be happening at this venue again. He wished he had something concrete against Marinde. Time was running out. The cops would be here soon.

"Did you notice anything weird with Sully and Sydney while you were there?" he asked. "Sully seems a little down. Rumor is that Sydney's mom doesn't want her involved with him."

"Now that you mention it, I did notice that Marinde looked annoyed whenever Sydney paid him attention." Cecelia tucked long auburn hair behind her ear. "And Sully was fidgety. Kept trying to rub something off his ski jacket. Does he always worry about stains or is that one of his nervous habits?"

"He brushes powdered sugar and donut crumbs off his clothes a lot."

Except that he just bought the donuts a few minutes ago, not while Cecelia was manning Cora's table. Evan glanced at Edna, then studied the condiments table. At that moment, an idea damn near exploded in his head. What if Sully had been trying to rub a mustard stain off his jacket? What if he'd picked it up after close proximity to Sydney, not her mother? Well, damn.

"Are you okay?" Cecelia asked. "You've got a funny look on your face."

"Yeah, fine. I just need to check something."

"Then I should go," Cecelia said. "Studying and packing awaits." She gave his hand a squeeze. "See you tonight. Can't wait to exchange gifts."

"Me too," he said, reminding himself yet again to pick up the amethyst necklace and earrings before closing time.

First things first, though, like the possibility that he'd been focusing on the wrong Marchant. It explained Sully's sombre mood, and why he hurried away when Evan asked Edna about the condiments table. What if Sully lied about seeing Marinde handle the water bottle? What if he'd seen Sydney instead? If that was true, then how in the hell could he persuade Sully to expose the girl of his dreams?

Chapter Ten

At the dispatch office, Evan panned the camera over the gym's parking lot, and then he saw it. Sully's old Corolla. He'd lied about going home. Evan had suspected as much or he wouldn't be scanning the lot in the first place. It was hard to believe that Sully had taken part in the mustard incident. Angry Santa, however, was another issue. If Sully had pulled that stunt, he could face some sort of reprimand. If he'd had something to do with the mustard incident, he'd risk being suspended or even expelled.

Evan hated the idea of giving Sully's name to the cops, but what was he supposed to do? If Okeyo found out that Evan had kept the truth from him to protect a friend, he'd lose his job and any chance of joining the RCMP. Man, he seriously needed to review the rest of the CCTV footage from Friday afternoon to see when Sully and Sydney left the building.

Short minutes later, Evan was cursing himself for not reviewing the footage earlier. The evidence he needed about Sydney Marchant's role in the mustard was right there on his screen.

The footage showed Marinde driving out of the parking lot at 4:36 p.m. She'd been alone and left just after the ambulance did. He remembered Marinde asking to carry her things out through the back entrance, which was why there'd been no sign of her departing through the front doors. But her daughter sure as hell had, and she hadn't been alone.

Evan was staring at footage of a laughing Sully and Sydney jogging out the front entrance at 4:58 p.m., eighteen minutes after Gran, Flo, and Agnes left the building, and seven minutes before Dave locked it up. He fast-forwarded the footage. No one except the guards had come and gone from the building the rest of the night.

Heavy footsteps trundled down the hall toward his door. Evan would recognize Okeyo's footsteps anywhere.

Okeyo stepped inside. "Dispatch confirmed that the police still haven't arrived. I guess the debacle on campus isn't a high priority, which is good. It'll give us time to prepare. Anymore progress?"

"Yeah." Evan showed Okeyo what he'd found. "The person who entered through the back on Saturday evening could have been Sydney Marchant. The height's about right." Evan paused. "When I brought the box of evidence to dispatch, I asked if that little bit of paper stuffed in the latch was still around, and it was. It matches the same lavender tissue paper the Marchants use to wrap their products."

"Great work." Okeyo moved to Evan's side of the desk and peered at the footage. "Did the girl work alone when she ruined those bowls?"

"Yes." Thank god, otherwise Sully could be facing criminal charges.

Sully might never forgive Evan for disclosing the truth, but letting his friend and Sydney get away with shit like that would be a betrayal to Gran and his boss.

"I spoke with my grandmother, who confirmed that Sydney drives a little silver compact, like the one that pulled up to the gym last night. We have a plate number."

"Excellent."

"Gran and a volunteer told me that Sydney and her mom suffered a fair bit of abuse from the father. The mother's planning to leave him and move away with Sydney right after Christmas."

Gran had been reluctant to discuss the Marchants, but after Evan told her about Sydney's involvement, she corroborated Edna's story about the family's situation.

"Marinde's husband used to help unload her products," he added. "Two years ago, though, he went off on a tirade and kicked her bins all over the parking lot, which is why Sydney now helps her. Everyone's relieved that the husband hasn't shown up since."

"I'm sorry for the women." Okeyo shook his head. "Your grandmother sure brought a shitstorm in with her, didn't she?"

Evan's face grew warm. "If I'd known, I wouldn't have recommended STT."

"Don't sweat it, Evan. You've solved

the crime spree."

Evan wished he felt better about it. "Listen, is it okay if I talk to Sully privately? I doubt he knows anything about the slashed bowls, but I think he suspects that Sydney had something to do with Cora's collapse and the mustard, and maybe even torching the tree." Evan cleared his throat. "I know that he's really troubled about this morning's events, so maybe he can persuade Sydney to own up. If he helps us out, I'm hoping he won't face any reprimand from STT. And Sully did put himself in danger to help us catch a killer last spring. That's got to count for something, right?"

Evan tried not to flinch under Okeyo's stare. The university's response to events, and especially Sully's actions, would depend on Okeyo's recommendations about disciplinary measures. The least Evan could do was find a way for Sully to stay in school.

"True," Okeyo answered. "But if he doesn't cooperate, there will be repercussions. Make sure he knows that, Evan."

"I will," Evan replied. "If Sully's expelled or even suspended, his father will probably disown him and kick him out on the street. And it sure won't help if the police wind up on his dad's doorstep, wanting to question Sully. His father is no better than Sydney's."

"I see." Okeyo paused. "All right. If he helps us, then I'll help him. But get dispatch to monitor his vehicle. If he leaves campus, I want to know about it right away."

As Okeyo left, Evan called Sully's number but it went to voice mail. He wasn't surprised.

Although two computer labs and the library were open for students on Sundays, food wasn't permitted in those rooms. Since Sully wasn't in his car or the gym, he would have to eat in the only cafeteria open today. Evan put on his jacket.

Five minutes later, he found Sully at a table in the corner, staring out the window. As he looked up, Evan saw a flicker of panic. Adopting a relaxed, unhurried manner, Evan eased into a chair.

"Decided to eat before heading home," Sully mumbled.

"Thought you might." Evan shifted in his chair. "You never told me what attracts you to Sydney so much."

Sully's quizzical glance turned to thoughtfulness. Evan couldn't tell if he was trying to decide how to answer or if he even knew the answer.

"She gets me. Knows what it's like to be pushed around."

Sully was one of the most compassionate human beings Evan knew. How he'd managed to stay that way after years of bullying at home and at school still amazed Evan. He had all the respect in the world for Sully and understood why he wanted to protect Sydney. Evan wasn't sure how to make Sully understand that by doing so, he was crossing a line that could ruin his future.

"Sully, the firefighters have evidence showing that someone deliberately set fire to the tree. They called the cops."

Another flicker of panic. Sully glanced at the entrance. The fight or flight urge had to be swelling inside him. And Sully was no fighter.

"So?" Sully blurted. "What's that got to do with me?"

"Nothing. But we do have footage of you and Sydney hurrying out of the gym Friday afternoon, after everyone else had left."

Sully jumped to his feet, nearly knocking the chair over. He reached for his coat, but Evan grabbed it from him. He spotted a small mustard smear near the base of the zipper. "How did the mustard get there?"

Sully wiped his mouth with the back of his hand. "You know me. Always making a mess."

Evan stared at his friend. "My theory is that Sydney got busy with the mustard while you taped the elf to Santa, although my guess is that the idea was Sydney's." Sully started to shake his head, but then stopped. Evan went on. "I'm thinking that you didn't know what she'd done until you saw the stain. Based on other things you probably witnessed this morning, you put two and two together."

Sully looked at the door again. "I'd better go home."

"Don't make me send the cops to your house, Sully." It wasn't fair but Evan had to push.

"I thought we were friends."

Sully's crestfallen face made Evan want to sink through the floor. "We are. But I have to wonder if you value Sydney's friendship more than mine right now, seeing as how you're covering for her." Evan paused. "Is she worth getting expelled over, Sully?"

His face paled. "The stain could have come from the condiment table," he said. "There's smears all over it."

Great. The guy was going to be stubborn about this. "Listen, I know how much it sucks to feel trapped, but you need to do what's right before someone else gets hurt."

Sully plunked into the chair. "Leave her alone, Evan."

"I can't, and the cops sure as hell won't. It's better if you tell me first, then maybe I can spin it somehow." Evan told him about the short person entering the gym Saturday evening, and Sydney's car in the parking lot.

Sully's mouth fell open. "I, uh…are you sure?"

"Afraid so. Did you now that she was planning to damage Walter's bowls?"

"No!" Sully fidgeted, then cleared his throat. "Okay, look, Sydney thought that messing with Santa would be funny. She found some tape and asked me to help, so I did. But then she told me that she forgot something at her mom's table and asked me to take over."

She must have planned to use Sully from the get-go. Did the girl have any feelings for him at all? "Did you see her handle the mustard bottle?"

"No, and I swear I didn't know anything about it, Evan. She was only gone a couple of minutes." Perspiration appeared on his brow. "Am I gonna get expelled?"

"Not if I can help it."

And if Okeyo could convince the STT disciplinary board that the elf prank was Sydney's idea. What worried Evan most was that Sydney would try to blame Sully for everything. Evan's phone rang. Gran. What now?

"Good news, Evvy. I just called the hospital and Cora's going to be fine."

"Excellent. Thanks for letting me know."

Evan was tempted to tell her about Sydney, but he was afraid that Gran would confront the girl. And since he didn't want to talk about her in front of Sully, he ended the call.

"What's excellent?" Sully asked, his tone suspicious.

"Cora Riddell's going to be okay."

"Good." Sully let out a long sigh.

His obvious relief gave Evan the opening he needed. "The cops are going to wonder how Cora managed to ingest a hallucinogen, possibly LSD. They might even see it as attempted murder, so I need to know if you saw Sydney touch Cora's water bottle."

Sully swallowed hard. The anguish on his friend's face told Evan that his suspicion was true.

"Her prints will be on it, Sully," he added. "Listen, I don't want to see Sydney busted. If you tell me everything, maybe we can figure out a way to help her."

"I can't believe that Syd intended to kill the old lady," Sully mumbled. "Probably just wanted her to leave the fair."

Evan wasn't so sure about that. "Tell me exactly what you saw."

Sully bit his lower lip, then said, "Syd took the bottle down the hall. A minute later, she came out of the bathroom and put it on Cora's table."

"Was that before or after the tree caught fire?"

"After," he answered. "The paramedics

were already with Cora."

"Did Sydney comment on the tree fire?"

Sully hesitated. "She said the fair's been a disorganized disaster from the start."

Because of her actions. Evan didn't recall seeing Sydney around during Cora and Gran's altercation. She must have slipped away, then planted the boxes in the tree and lit the candles while everyone was focused on Cora and Gran. Once all the attention switched to the fire, she would have rinsed out Cora's water bottle.

"You should also know that Syd took a lighter out of her sweater pocket and dropped it in her backpack. She doesn't smoke." Sully plunked his elbows on the table and clamped his hands over his temples. "What am I going to do, Evan?"

"I don't know, bud."

"She can't go to jail!"

His desperation worried Evan. "I doubt that Gran will press charges about the fire." Cora, however, was another matter. "Think Sydney's mother knows what's going on?"

"Dunno. Even if she did, she'd probably cover for her."

So, how would the Marchants react when the cops came marching up to them?

Another thought occurred to Evan. "Sully, have you seen a small hatchet with an oak handle at the Marchant's table, or in Sydney's backpack?"

"No." His eyebrows rose. "Why?"

"I'm pretty sure that Sydney used it on Walter's bowls. It'd be good if we find it before the cops do." Evan didn't add that he wanted to get the hatchet as far away from the girl as possible.

"I'll go look," Sully said.

"I'll go with you."

"No, I can do it. That way I can talk to Sydney."

"Sorry, man. Okeyo would be furious if I asked you to do what I'm supposed to handle. But if you want to talk to her privately first, I'll hang back a bit. Just know that I need to be there."

Sully's already pale face took on a greenish tinge. "I feel sick. I've got to use the can."

"I'll wait outside. And Sully?" He glanced over his shoulder as he trudged toward the men's room. "Don't call Sydney. If she knows I'm onto her, it could cause a shitload of trouble."

"Fine. Whatever."

Evan wasn't completely sure that Sully would honour his request about the phone, but confiscating it would do more harm than good. Where the hell were the cops anyway?

Evan called Okeyo. He stepped away from the door so Sully couldn't overhear. "I know who's responsible for everything." Evan kept things brief and to the point.

"Great work," Okeyo said. "As soon as the police arrive, we'll meet in the gym. And don't let Sully out of your sight. We should have guards keep an eye on the girl."

"Too many uniforms could freak her out," Evan said. "I'll text Felix and ask him to discreetly watch Sydney. I could also ask Cecelia to pop over. Since she's not security staff, she might be able to get closer."

"I suppose that's all right. But make it clear that she's not to endanger herself. Sydney strikes me as unstable and unpredictable."

"Agreed." Evan called Cecelia. "Hey, could you head back to the fair? I need help with something fast."

"Actually, I'm still here. Decided to grab a coffee with Martha, but she had to get back to the registration desk. She looks exhausted, Evan. I think she's afraid that more bad things will happen before this day's over."

"She could be right." After he told Cecelia about Sydney, he said, "Can you see what she's up to, without getting too close? It'd be better if she didn't see you at all. I'll stay on the line until you spot her."

Evan glanced at the bathroom door. Sully was taking a long time. He couldn't have taken off as there were no windows in there.

"I see Sydney. She and her mom are busy with customers," Cecelia said. "Everything seems fine. She's not on the phone."

"Good."

Sully emerged from the bathroom, looking depressed and still green. "Stomach's okay for the moment."

"Uh-oh. Evan?" Cecelia whispered. "You'd better get over here. A cop just walked through the door."

Chapter Eleven

Evan and Sully raced into the lobby, where Gran was talking to a constable. Steve and Felix stayed close by. Janelle also stood close enough to hear every word.

"There's my grandson, Evvy," Gran said. "He's in charge of security."

"I'm second-in-command," he told the cop. "The man in charge will join us shortly."

Evan had radioed Okeyo on his way to the vehicle. Okeyo had alerted all guards to a possible incident in the gym. Steve, Felix, and one other were already gathering, their expressions a mix of curiosity, pensiveness, and excitement. This was one of the few times Evan hadn't seen disdain or smugness on Steve's face. He was the one who looked excited.

"Are you here alone," Evan asked the cop, "or are there others?"

"My partner's in the gym," he answered.

One other. Evan wasn't sure that would be enough.

"They're here about the fire and what happened to Cora," Gran remarked, not looking the least bit happy.

Sully darted toward the gym.

"Sully!" Evan called, but was ignored.

"Is that guy involved in the incidents?" the cop asked, watching Sully.

"No, but he's a friend of the girl who's responsible for all of it. She's the daughter of one of the vendors."

Gran's eyes widened. "Sydney?"

"Yes."

"Oh, dear." Gran looked dazed. "Why?"

"Let's find out," the cop said. "Where's the vendor located?"

"It's the *Natural Scents* table," Gran answered, showing him the floor plan. "On the right side of the gym, at the other end of the room."

Evan turned to Steve and Felix. "Can you two watch the back entrance? We don't want Sydney leaving, but stay well away from her."

"What does she look like?" Steve asked.

"Short, pudgy, and wearing an ugly Christmas sweater. If you can't see her, ask Cecelia to point her out. Tell her I said she should leave the area right now."

For once, Steve didn't give him any trouble, but merely followed Felix inside the gym.

"Let's go," the officer said.

Evan led the way, noting that the second cop stood just inside the door near the front, surveying the gym. Mercifully, there were fewer shoppers now. The two officers quietly conferred with one another as Okeyo entered the room. His commanding, six-foot-three presence caused people to step back.

"Have you briefed the officers?" Okeyo asked Evan.

"About Sydney, yes. But not about the missing hatchet."

"Then you'd better do so."

After Evan introduced Okeyo, he told the cops about the hatchet.

"Is this girl likely to become aggressive when she sees us?" the first constable asked.

Evan hesitated. "It's possible." He worried that Sully would try to help her.

The second cop said he would call for backup and approach the back entrance from outside.

"What about the mother?" the cop asked. "Is she a problem?"

"I don't think she's in on this," Evan replied, noting that Gran was listening. "Nor do I think she's violent."

"But make no mistake," Gran said, "Marinde will do whatever it takes to protect her daughter."

While the second cop headed back through the lobby, the first cop started down the aisle. Evan hoped he could keep Sully from doing something stupid. He spotted Sully near the Marchants' table. His friend was fidgeting as he watched Sydney chatting with customers.

"Is that her?" the constable asked Evan, his stare fixed on Sydney.

"Yes," he replied, noting that Sully was now aware of their presence, and looking mortified.

The customers left the table about the

same time Sydney and Marinde noticed the approaching constable. Confusion crossed Marinde's face, but not Sydney's. Her cheeks were turning crimson as Sully reached for her. She shook him off.

"Sydney Marchant?" the constable asked.

"Yes."

"We'd like a word, please."

"What about?" Sydney asked petulantly.

The cop paused. "Could you step out from the table?"

"No. I have to help my mother."

Marinde frowned at the cop. "What do you want with my daughter?"

The cop turned to her. "How old is your daughter, Mrs. Marchant?"

"I'll be nineteen in three weeks," Sydney answered for her. "And why should I talk to you?"

"It would be better if we spoke privately."

"Anything you say to her, you do so in my presence," Marinde said.

"We don't have to talk to them at all," Sydney shot back.

"Syd." Sully grabbed her hand. "It's okay."

Sydney tried to shake her hand free, but he wouldn't let go.

"I thought you were my friend," she said to him.

"I am."

"Then get me out of here!"

"I can't." The misery in Sully's flushed expression made Evan's stomach clench. "Evan's figured some stuff out."

"Bullshit! He's not that smart!"

"Standing right here," Evan mumbled.

"He is, Syd. Trust me. He knows about Santa."

Sydney gaped at him. "You told?"

"He figured it out, and I'm not good with pressure."

"It was just a stupid joke." She wrenched her hand free of his. "And it was your idea anyway."

"That's not true!" Sully gaped at her. "How can you say that?"

Sydney's mouth quivered. "I'm sorry. You're a good guy, and I really do like you."

Gran stepped out from behind Evan.

"Sydney, did you squirt mustard on Flo and Cora's tables?" she asked.

Both the cop and Sydney glared at Gran.

Evan figured he was about to tell Gran to leave when Sydney blurted, "You're all losers!"

"Sydney, mind your manners!" Marinde gaped at daughter. "And why would she ask you that?"

"I don't know! Her ass-hat grandson probably got that stupid idea."

"Still standing right here," Evan said. "Sully saw you pick up Cora's water bottle and take it down the hall."

"So what?" Her voice rose.

"He saw you slip a lighter in your backpack," Evan stated calmly. "We also have camera footage of you entering the building through the back entrance on Saturday night. Your Echo's license plate was recorded too."

Sydney bent down and reached under the table. When she stood, she was gripping the hatchet with both hands.

"Don't!" Sully yelled. "Put it down!"

A second later, she bolted down the hallway.

"Stop!" Sully went after her.

The constable said something into his radio mic as he too ran. Evan followed. Steve and Felix stood at the end of the hall, their eyes wide as Sydney drew closer.

She raised the hatchet. "Move!"

Steve flung the door open, and he and Felix took off.

"Stop!" the constable yelled. "Drop the weapon right now!"

"Sydney!" Sully shouted. "Don't! They'll hurt you. Let me help!"

Evan followed them outside, into the light, chilly rainfall. Sydney ran toward Cecelia who was several yards ahead.

"Cecelia, run!" Evan yelled.

Cecelia spun around, gaped at Sydney, then bolted toward the dorm.

The second cop who'd been walking toward the back of the building darted forward, placing himself between Cecelia and Sydney. Cecelia ran until she'd reached a safe distance, but she didn't leave.

Both cops raised their weapons. The cop nearest Evan held a Taser. "Drop the hatchet, now!"

"Sydney!" Marinde screamed. She tried to approach Sydney, but the first cop held her back. "Let me go! My daughter won't hurt me!"

Two more patrol cars screeched to a stop. Officers jumped out and went for their weapons. Sydney turned and raced toward Birch stream. A footbridge over the stream would take her to the sports field. Beyond that was marshland, and to the left, forest. She had nowhere else to go. Sydney must have realized that she was trapped because she slowed to a stop. Hatchet still in hand, she stood there sobbing.

"Put the weapon down," the cop ordered.

"Sydney!" Marinde called out. "I know you're angry, but this isn't the way, honey."

"Please, Syd!" Sully pleaded. "Do what they say."

"Your mother's dead!" Sydney yelled at him. "You don't know what it's like to watch your mom being humiliated every day! First by Dad and then those incompetent fair fuckers!"

She nodded toward Gran who stood next to Evan. Out the corner of his eye, Evan saw Janelle and Agnes.

"Martha was supposed to make things better," Sydney went on. "But she wouldn't listen to us any more than the other bitch did!"

Evan turned to Janelle. Leaning on her cane with both hands, Janelle stared at

Sydney with a blank expression.

"Sydney," Marinde said. "It's okay. None of this matters because we're leaving town."

"It's *not* okay! Every time we do these fairs, Cora makes your life so miserable that you can't even sleep." Tears streamed down her face. "I'm sick of it!"

"It's not your problem, honey, it's mine," Marinde said, choking back a sob. "I should have stood up to them. Please, baby, put the hatchet down. We'll work this out."

Tears and gut-wrenching sobs caused Sydney to shake so hard that the hatchet fell on the ground. The cops rushed forward, ordering Sully back. Within seconds, Sydney was restrained, the hatchet retrieved and secured.

Gran approached the constable they'd been speaking with. "I'm not pressing charges about the mischief."

Evan doubted that Flo would either, but Cora? Cecelia came up to Evan and took his hand. He gave her a reassuring squeeze.

"This is partly on you, Martha, and Janelle!" Marinde shouted. "If you two had been better listeners, none of this would have happened!"

Gran's face reddened. Even Janelle managed to look somewhat remorseful. Agnes stepped forward and put her arm around Gran.

"I'm so terribly sorry, Marinde," Gran said. "I just figured you could handle Cora better than anyone."

"Why? Because I didn't curse and complain and carry on like the other vendors?" Marinde swiped at the tears cascading down her face. "If that's the only way to get your attention, then you should never have been put in charge!"

Marinde hurried over to the officers who were escorting Sydney to a patrol car. While Okeyo spoke with another constable, Gran walked up to Evan and Cecelia.

"Don't listen to her, Martha," Agnes said. "You did the best you could in a tough situation."

Gran patted her hand, then turned to Evan. "Thank you, son." She hugged him. "If you hadn't solved this thing, who knows how much more damage that poor girl would have done."

He saw the guilt in her eyes and knew that she felt as responsible as Marinde wanted her to. "You're welcome." Evan couldn't help feeling sorry for her, for the Marchants and Sully too.

"I guess her craft fair savings will have to be spent on lawyers," Agnes remarked.

Gran nodded and sighed. "We should do something to help."

"No," Agnes replied. "This is their family, their problem."

Gran peered at her. "You sure about that?" She headed back inside, as did the others.

"Sounds to me like Sydney will need a lot of counseling," Cecelia said. "Maybe they really should leave the area. Start fresh somewhere else."

"Sully won't be happy." Evan saw him standing by the patrol vehicle, gazing at Sydney who was pressing her palm against the glass and peering at him.

"For whatever it's worth," Cecelia said, "I think she cares about him."

"Maybe." But Sully's taste in women was definitely questionable.

"I've really got to get some studying and packing done," she said. "See you at eight. Can't wait to exchange our gifts."

The gifts! Shit! "Me too." He wanted to kiss her, but with Okeyo nearby, he didn't dare.

Evan headed inside. Reports and debriefing could wait. Right now, a sparkly amethyst necklace and earring set were waiting for him.

~ * ~

If you enjoyed this book, please consider writing a short review and posting it on your favorite review site. Reviews are very helpful to other readers and are greatly appreciated by authors, especially me. When you post a review, drop me an email and let me know and I may feature part of it on my blog/site. Thank you.

Debra

Message from the Author

Dear Reader,

Like many of my stories, this novella was inspired by my real-life experiences as a vendor at many Christmas craft fairs. To be honest, I've never seen the level of rivalry, and certainly not the violence, that I've created in this novella—and hopefully never will!

In this second Evan Dunstan installment, Evan certainly has his hands full. While I was training as a security guard through the Justice Institute of British Columbia, the instructor said that a lot about security could be boring...until something happens. And things always happen to Evan.

I owe a big thanks to incredibly the talented writers who gave me invaluable feedback on this book. I'd again like to thank Cheryl Tardif for her support. It's been a pleasure to work with her wonderful team at Imajin.

If you enjoyed this novella, I'd really appreciate a review. And please feel free to contact me at debra_kong@telus.net with comments or questions.

I'm currently working on the third Evan Dunstan mystery. This book (as yet untitled) takes place close Halloween, where, ghost, witches, and zombies invade Evan's workplace. This will be his most challenging mystery yet!

About the Author

Debra Purdy Kong's volunteer experiences, criminology diploma, and various jobs, inspired her to write mysteries set in BC's Lower Mainland. Her employment as a campus security patrol and communications officer provide the background for her Evan Dunstan mysteries, as well as her Casey Holland transit security novels.

Debra has published short stories in a variety of genres as well as personal essays, and articles for publications such as *Chicken Soup for the Bride's Soul, B.C. Parent Magazine,* and *The Vancouver Sun.* She assists as a facilitator for the Creative Writing Program through Port Moody Recreation, and has presented workshops and talks for organizations that include Mensa and Beta Sigma Phi. She is a long-time member of Crime Writers of Canada.

Look for her blog at http://writetype.blogspot.ca More information about Debra and her books is at:

www.debrapurdykong.com You can also find her on Twitter: https://twitter.com/DebraPurdyKong & Facebook: www.facebook.com/debra.purdykong

Be the first to know when Debra Purdy Kong's next book is finally available! Follow Debra at: https://www.bookbub.com/authors/debra-purdy-kong to receive new release and discount alerts.

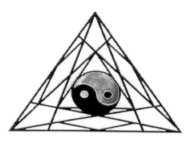

IMAJIN BOOKS®
Quality fiction beyond your wildest dreams

For your next eBook or paperback purchase,
please visit:

www.imajinbooks.com

www.imajinbooks.blogspot.com

www.twitter.com/imajinbooks

www.facebook.com/imajinbooks

IMAJIN QWICKIES®
www.ImajinQwickies.com

82998054R00085

Made in the USA
Columbia, SC
22 December 2017